# BEYOND EQUATION

## A JOURNEY THROUGH MATHEMATICS AND THE HEART

PRITAM NANDI

Dedicated to the memory of my late father,

Mr. Bimal Nandi,

whose enduring love and guidance shape every word in this book.
Your legacy lives on in these pages. Forever missed and forever loved.

Pritam Nandi

# Contents

# Prologue

In a calm village surrounded by fields, where time moved gently like leaves in the wind, a special story began. It's not just about a man going from studying by lantern light to big universities; it's a tale woven with strong determination, dreams, and the lasting warmth of connections.

This story is about Rajesh, a young man with big dreams that went beyond his simple start. His journey is set against a backdrop of love, guidance, and unwavering support from those who believed in his hidden talents. Most importantly, this story is a celebration of people's inner strength and how dreams, when cared for by hard work and supportive friends, can really come true.

So, let's start this adventure and see how Rajesh's life unfolds. His story is full of love, friendship, and the lasting influence of a father's memory that goes far beyond each part of the tale.

# Acknowledgements

A heartfelt thank you to my late father, Mr. Bimal Nandi, whose memory is the foundation of this narrative. His influence, wisdom, and unwavering belief in dreams have shaped every word on these pages.

To my beloved mother and family and friends, your support has been a beacon of strength. Your encouragement fueled the writing process, and I am grateful for the love that surrounds me.

# CHAPTER ONE

# Beginning of A Journey Beyond the Fields

Rajesh looked out at the endless fields of swaying wheat, its golden stalks stretching to the horizons in rippling waves. Every creak of the bullock carts and chirp of birds in the nearby forest had a meaning if you bothered to pay attention. Suddenly, dark clouds gathered overhead, casting a shadow on the once-calm landscape. The distant rumble of thunder echoed through the air, and as raindrops began to pour down, Rajesh's urgency increased. With each step, he hurried through the mud, his heart beating fast with the growing storm, determined to reach his destination before the rain unleashed its full force.

This, his beloved village of Panchpota, was all Rajesh had ever known. From dawn till dusk, he trailed after his mother Shanti through their daily chores, eager to lend small hands. Yet his greatest joy came not from work, but exploration—weaving amid the crops to observe insects at play, or lingering by the river spotting shapes in its currents while others fetched water.

Rajesh's gifts had not gone unnoticed. "That boy thinks

more than most grown men!" the villagers would say, chuckling. But only one took his talents seriously: Professor Rao, the graying schoolmaster who taught all the local children. While others saw a scrawny troublemaker, the Professor glimpsed a brilliant spark—and vowed to fan its flame.

On weekends, he often invited Rajesh to his humble quarters, sharing books far beyond the village textbooks. "What patterns do you perceive here, my boy?" he would ask, setting Rajesh's mind ablaze with puzzles. Through these sessions, Rajesh learned not only letters but also life's deeper mysteries. He began to envision vast libraries beyond Panchpota, their pages holding answers to every question. This, he knew, was his destiny—to seek knowledge wherever it may lead. Rajesh thrived under Professor Rao's guidance. By then, he had mastered multiplication tables, much to the schoolmistress Mrs. Ghosh's astonishment. But as the years passed, it became clear Rajesh had a gift beyond typical village lessons.

When examining patterns in numbers, shapes emerged before Rajesh with breathtaking clarity. Equations unraveled their mysteries at a glance. While classmates struggled over decimals, Rajesh sailed past such basics, craving tougher problems like a parched man who thirsts for water. His teachers happily obliged, devising puzzles to continue stretching his remarkable mind.

Soon Rajesh grasped algebraic concepts usually taught years beyond primary level. Derivations and integrals that left university graduates perplexed unwound simply under Rajesh's scrutiny. Word of the village prodigy spread, and people flocked to witness the boy solve problems in minutes that had stumped professors for months.

"A mind like his comes but once in a generation," Professor Rao told Rajesh's beaming mother, as crowds applauded another of Rajesh's lightning victories. But amid the praise, Rajesh remained thoughtful, aware deeper depths of mathematical wonder awaited exploration if only his gifts might progress beyond Panchpota's fields. His destiny called to lands where, perhaps, similar souls gathered seeking the next discovery. The day dawned like any other in Professor Rao's cramped classroom. Yet as Rajesh took his usual seat, an unfamiliar gleam lit the teacher's eyes.

After dismissing the others for recess, Professor Rao motioned Rajesh over. "You've come so far, my boy. But a mind as gifted as yours was never meant for village lessons alone."

Rajesh's breath caught. Always the Professor had praised his progress, yet never suggested greater heights. "What are you saying, sir?"

Professor Rao smiled. "The headmaster and I believe you're ready for university, Rajesh. Your grasp of equations exceeds students ten years your senior."

University—the place of Rajesh's dreams, where knowledge's depths might be plumbed. Yet how could such splendors be meant for a poor villager's son? "But the fees, sir. And to leave Amma and the fields..."

His teacher's hand squeezed reassurance. "Do not worry

over costs. With my support and your scholarships, all will be arranged. As for your family, they will understand this is God's plan for you."

Professor Rao's confidence kindled hope in Rajesh's heart, where doubt had taken root. If his mentor said the world awaited, perhaps it was so. Rajesh smiled, a new future unfolding before his eyes. This was only the beginning., That evening, as the family broke bread together by lantern light, Rajesh broke his news. He expected opposition—his father Keshav was a man of the soil, unchanged by years.

Sure enough, upon hearing of the university, Keshav snorted. "More schooling? Waste of time and money, when our land awaits your hands. Who'll till the fields while you're off in fancy cities playing with numbers?"

Rajesh's mother Shanti shot her husband a pleading look. "Let the boy speak, Keshav. Professor Rao believes in him."

Keshav glowered but fell silent. Rajesh met his father's eyes steadily. "My place is not here, Abba. My gift is for higher things."

"Gift?! Fool's talk," Keshav growled. But Rajesh was undeterred. Through the coming weeks, he worked twice as hard to prove himself a dutiful son, even as Professor Rao smoothed the path ahead.

In the end, it was Shanti who understood. "Go with God, my son. Make your people proud." Her blessing released the last of Rajesh's doubts. Though his father refused to speak at seeing him off, Rajesh boarded the bus with resolve. A new chapter was beginning, no matter the cost. His destiny called him forth. Rajesh plunged into university life with fervor. Late into the night, he pored over thick tomes by guttering candlelight, voraciously absorbing all branches of mathematics. While others struggled, equations danced before Rajesh's eyes like poetry.

Algebra melted away puzzles with but a glance, as though he perceived formulas' underlying harmonies. Professors marveled at this orphaned villager solving problems in moments that had stumped even themselves. Word of the stellar student from Panchpota spread.

Yet Rajesh remained humble. As dawn light filtered into his sparse quarters, he gave thanks - not for gifts setting him apart, but for each discovery bringing him closer to the divine mysteries unifying all existence. His commitment inspired peers, who admired his dual brilliance and character.

At the village, Shanti lit lamps in the little shrine, praying God bless her son's journey. And bless him he did - within a year, Rajesh emerged top of the university through sheer dint of talent and toil. His future, once uncertain, now blossomed with infinite potential. This was only the start of his transformation, The day of Rajesh's home visit arrived. Around the hearth that evening, between mouthfuls of daal and rice, he spoke of the university's wonders. Spellbound, his sisters hung on every word.

But Keshav remained stern. "More schooling won't fill mouths or plow fields."

Shanti shot back, "His gift must grow, not wither here!"

Tension sizzled as siblings watched their elders argue. Rajesh swallowed hard, then said softly, "My place is among thinkers, seeking humanity's advance."

Keshav slammed his bowl down. "Ungrateful boy! I gave you life yet you abandoned me—your blood!"

Shanti cried, "He brings us pride, not abandonment!"

As anger swelled, Rajesh stood. "My path is chosen. Support or oppose me, that matters not—I go to claim my destiny."

With hardened eyes, Keshav turned away. A long silence fell.

Then Shanti embraced her son. "May God light your way. Go—and fulfill the promise in your soul."

Her faith rekindled Rajesh's. Though his father refused the promise of tomorrow, tomorrow would come—borne on Rajesh's unflinching spirit. That night, as others slept, Shanti spoke to Rajesh beneath starry skies. Your father is a man of the soil -- he knows no other way. But I see the scholar in you, just as Professor Rao does. Go, with my blessing and support.

Arjun, Rajesh's brother-in-law, emerged and added, Keshav will come around, as village ways fall to new times. Earn your degree - I shall tend the fields so your duty is met.

Tears glistened in Rajesh's eyes. Were it not for your faith,

I'd falter. But with hearts like yours at my side, how can I not succeed?

Shanti embraced him. We are but bits of starstuff, all of us connected though distances or disagreements may pull us apart. Stay true to your light and it will guide you home in time, as surely as these stars light the sky each night.

Fortified by their belief despite his father's opposition, Rajesh's resolve hardened like steel. With all said, he sought sleep, dreaming of the knowledge awaiting him beyond the fields' rim come sunrise. His journey was beginning. Rajesh's big day dawned. As he walked the dusty road to the exam hall, butterflies swirled in his stomach. What if despite years of study, he still fell short? Worse - what if failure proved his father right?

Steeling his nerves, Rajesh said a prayer to Saraswati, Goddess of Knowledge. Her blessings had carried him this far. Within the crowded hall, he sat determined to give his best.

The test began. Pencils scratched as others sweated over questions. But for Rajesh, answers slipped easily from mind to page like silk threads drawn through a loom. Derivations flowed; integrals unraveled. Before long, he emerged into the bright sun, papers complete. Now there was naught to do but wait and pray his efforts merited reward. Weeks seemed to crawl by. Then one afternoon, Shanti appeared clutching a letter. She hugged Rajesh tightly. "You've done it, my son. University is yours!"

Joy and relief washed over him in waves. His dream, once

so distant, had become reality through perseverance. That evening at the little shrine, Rajesh thanked the Goddess whose grace had opened this new chapter. His journey was only beginning, as bright futures dawned on the horizon. That evening, the village came alive with lights and music for the annual harvest fair. As families flocked to stalls laden with sweets and toys, Rajesh helped his mother in the fields, thinking of days now past.

Each year at the fair, he had solved puzzles under colored lanterns to earn trinkets for sisters, dazzling onlookers with his gifts. How distant and small his village seemed now - yet its people remained dear as family.

Shanti smiled at her pensive son. Go, enjoy yourself! You've earned respite from these old joys before new dreams call you hence.

Rajesh hugged her close. Part of him would always belong with soil and folk who gave him roots. Yet tomorrow beckoned and, with it, chances to make them proud through knowledge. As fireworks lit the sky in an exploding rainbow, Rajesh gave thanks for the blessings guiding him toward horizons barely imagined from these familiar fields. His journey was only beginning.

# CHAPTER TWO

# A Village Prodigy's Triumph and Challenges

Rajesh paced the courtyard, glancing up at the sky as if somehow the letter containing his future would descend from the heavens. Each day that passed without a response increased his anxiety, a swarm of doubts rising within him like monsoon clouds.

All his efforts over the past year came down to this moment. If he didn't receive acceptance, what would he do? Return in defeat to Panchpota and live out his days in the fields, his brilliance ignored and wasted? The thought was unbearable.

He heard the scrape of chalk on slate from within the house - his mother brushing away the dust of past lessons as she prepared for the new term. Though outwardly calm, did she share his worries in private moments?
Had she also begun to lose hope?

A cawing crow interrupted his musings. Rajesh shielded his eyes from the late afternoon sun peering over rooftops and watched as the bird swooped out of the sky, something clutched in its beak. As it approached him, the object fell free - a crisp white envelope, unmarked but for his name. His breath caught in his throat. This was it. His fate had arrived, borne on black wings.

Hands trembling, Rajesh bent to pick up the letter. Behind him, the wooden threshold creaked - had his mother sensed the moment too? Steeling himself, he broke the seal and unfolded the paper within, finding the words that would change his life... Rajesh's eyes scanned the page, hardly believing the words that danced before him.

"We are pleased to inform you..."

A roar rose up in his ears, deafening all else. For a moment, he feared he may swoon from the ferocity of emotions battling within - joy, relief, disbelief, and such mountainous pride that he thought his heart might burst from its confines.

He had done it. Against all odds, defying even his father's doubts, he had secured his place at the university. Rajesh was the first in his family, the first from Panchpota even, to attend an institution of higher learning. The magnitude of this achievement threatened to overwhelm him.

His daze was broken by a small gasp. Whirling around, he found his mother behind him, hands pressed to her mouth in astonishment and delight. Wordlessly, he held out the letter for her eyes, beaming as fresh tears of wonder and gratitude welled in hers. Without a thought for propriety, she pulled him into an embrace, both laughing and crying together as the sun sank below the treeline in a blaze of red and gold. This night, the lamps of every home would shine all the brighter, for their son, their brother, their friend, had proven that no dream is too great when nurtured by courage, intellect and community. Rajesh's journey was just beginning. Here is the beginning of Chapter 2:

Rajesh paced around his small bedroom, nerves getting the better of him. Any day now, the university's letter would arrive informing him of whether his application was successful. So much was riding on this moment.

For weeks, he had replayed the entrance exam in his head, analyzing every question and answer. Had he made a foolish mistake somewhere? Missed interpreting an important concept? He couldn't bear the thought of falling short now, not after all the sacrifices his family had made to support him.

Hearing his mother in the kitchen, Rajesh went to help with breakfast, hoping the mindless tasks would distract him from his worries. But they swirled endlessly in his mind. What if despite his best efforts, it still wasn't enough? If he didn't get accepted, all his dreams of continuing his education would be shattered.

Just then, a knock sounded at the front door. Rajesh's heart leapt into his throat. Could it be...? Rushing over, he flung the door open to find the postman holding a thick envelope bearing the university's seal. With trembling hands, Rajesh took it from him. This was it, the moment of truth. After months of waiting, his future was contained within this letter. Taking a steadying breath, Rajesh broke the seal with tremoring fingers, unfolded the paper within and began to read... Rajesh scanned the page eagerly, barely able to believe his eyes as he took in the congratulatory words. He had been accepted. All those hours of study, the sacrifices of his family—it had all paid off.

A gasp escaped him as the realization struck: he would be the first person from his village to attend university. A wave of emotion overcame Rajesh—pride at having achieved what no one else from Panchpota ever had, gratitude for those who believed in him when others did not. But mingled with it was uncertainty—he knew moving to the big city would come with many challenges. Could he succeed where no one expected him to?

Hearing his exclamation, his mother came rushing in. "What is it, beta? Have you heard from the university?" At Rajesh's beaming nod, she clasped her hands in delight. "Ah, I knew my talented son would pass! Look at you, making your poor mother so proud. Just wait till I tell the whole village—Professor Rao will be thrilled at the news!"

As she bustled off to begin preparations to celebrate, Rajesh stared wonderingly at the letter once more. A new path was unfolding before him, one that would test him in ways he couldn't yet fathom. But he was determined to make the most of this opportunity and fulfill the hopes of all those who encouraged him to shoot for the stars. Rajesh rushed outside, clutching the letter tight, desperate to share his joy. His mother had already spread the word, for a small crowd had gathered by their home, wearing smiles of anticipation.

every question and answer. Had he made a foolish mistake somewhere? Missed interpreting an important concept? He couldn't bear the thought of falling short now, not after all the sacrifices his family had made to support him.

Hearing his mother in the kitchen, Rajesh went to help with breakfast, hoping the mindless tasks would distract him from his worries. But they swirled endlessly in his mind. What if despite his best efforts, it still wasn't enough? If he didn't get accepted, all his dreams of continuing his education would be shattered.

Just then, a knock sounded at the front door. Rajesh's heart leapt into his throat. Could it be...? Rushing over, he flung the door open to find the postman holding a thick envelope bearing the university's seal. With trembling hands, Rajesh took it from him. This was it, the moment of truth. After months of waiting, his future was contained within this letter. Taking a steadying breath, Rajesh broke the seal with tremoring fingers, unfolded the paper within and began to read... Rajesh scanned the page eagerly, barely able to believe his eyes as he took in the congratulatory words. He had been accepted. All those hours of study, the sacrifices of his family—it had all paid off.

A gasp escaped him as the realization struck: he would be the first person from his village to attend university. A wave of emotion overcame Rajesh—pride at having achieved what no one else from Panchpota ever had, gratitude for those who believed in him when others did not. But mingled with it was uncertainty—he knew moving to the big city would come with many challenges. Could he succeed where no one expected him to?

Hearing his exclamation, his mother came rushing in. "What is it, beta? Have you heard from the university?" At Rajesh's beaming nod, she clasped her hands in delight. "Ah, I knew my talented son would pass! Look at you, making your poor mother so proud. Just wait till I tell the whole village—Professor Rao will be thrilled at the news!"

As she bustled off to begin preparations to celebrate, Rajesh stared wonderingly at the letter once more. A new path was unfolding before him, one that would test him in ways he couldn't yet fathom. But he was determined to make the most of this opportunity and fulfill the hopes of all those who encouraged him to shoot for the stars. Rajesh rushed outside, clutching the letter tight, desperate to share his joy. His mother had already spread the word, for a small crowd had gathered by their home, wearing smiles of anticipation.

As soon as his brother-in-law Devraj spotted him, he called out, "Well, don't keep us in suspense! What does it say?" Rajesh beamed. "I'm in. The university accepted me."

A raucous cheer went up, and in an instant, Rajesh was engulfed in hugs and claps on his back. "I knew my boy would make it," his mother proclaimed proudly, eyes glistening. "You deserve this."

Devraj pumped his hand vigorously. "Congratulations, little brother. I always said you were destined for great things." His support over the years had been invaluable - without him and Ami, this day may not have come.

Soon the whole village had gathered, offering heartfelt

felicitations. But it was Professor Rao's appreciation that moved Rajesh most. His mentor ruffled his hair fondly. "Now the real work begins. Make the most of this, my boy. You'll do us all proud."

As night fell on celebrations, Rajesh knew that with the love and trust of his village behind him, he was ready to take his first steps into a brightness future. That evening, as others congregated at Rajaesh's home with gifts and good wishes, his father chose to remain absent. While Ami tried dismissing it, Rajesh knew his acceptance brought little joy to the family patriarch.

Later, as they shared a simple celebratory meal, Rajesh broached the subject carefully. "Father, now that I've been accepted, will you—"

But Ramchandra cut him off sternly. "Wasting time and money on education you don't need. Your place is here in the fields." Rajesh's shoulders slumped, but his brother-in-law Devraj placed a comforting hand on his back.

"Whatever you require for your studies, consider it done," Devraj assured gently. Rajesh met his mother's sad smile with grateful eyes, knowing her support was what truly mattered. Though Ramchandra's disapproval stung, it would not deter him from pursuing the future meant for him. With his village's blessing and faith in his abilities, Rajesh was determined to make them all proud through his accomplishments alone. The path ahead was uncertain, but with devotion and diligence, he would find a way. With his father refusing to contribute anything, the financial burden of Rajesh's education now fell solely on his mother Ami and

Devraj. They quietly sold a portion of their land to cover the exorbitant tuition fees. Rajesh tried easing their burden by borrowing books from Professor Rao instead of buying new ones. But travel and living expenses in the city were unavoidable. Each day, he saw how his dreams stretched his family's meagre savings to the brink.

One evening, Rajesh found Ami and Devraj going over accounts, troubled expressions on their faces. "How much more do you need for the term?" asked Devraj with a sigh. Rajesh told them reluctantly, seeing their weary smiles.

"We'll manage, beta," said Ami, ever resilient. But Rajesh heard the unspoken cost - it would leave them struggling for months. His heart clenched with love, guilt and determination. He swore silently to make the sacrifice worth it through his success.

From that day on, Rajesh redoubled his efforts, working odd jobs to lessen the burden on his benefactors. Though the path was difficult, he drew strength from their unstinting support in the face of opposition. It was a debt he aimed to repay through fulfilling the dreams they believed in., As the morning of departure arrived, Rajesh's village gathered at the train station to bid him farewell. Amid tears and goodbyes, his mother adjusted his collar with quivering hands. "Be safe, beta. Study hard."

Devraj clasped his shoulder. "The city may dazzle you, but remember where you come from. We're proud of you." Professor Rao smiled fondly. "You've come a long way from my littlest pupil. Now go spread your wings."

As the train whistle blew, Rajesh hugged his family tightly, feeling like a fledgling leaving the nest for the first time. He was anxious about the urban world awaiting him, but excitement simmered within too. A new chapter was beginning.

Boarding with an unsteady breath, Rajesh waved to the gathering from his window seat until Panchpota receded into the horizon. For the first time, he was striking out on his own, venturing into the unknown alone. Yet in his heart travelled the countless hopes and blessings of all who made this precious new beginning possible. Now, the real journey commenced. As Rajesh stepped onto the university platform, the city's frenetic energy overwhelmed him. Walking among bustling crowds, he felt conspicuously rustic in his village attire.

At the campus gates, rows of imposing buildings towered overhead, more magnificent than any structure he'd seen. Students milled everywhere in fashionable clothes, engaged in lively chatter. Compared to their worldly sophistication, Rajesh had never felt more out of his depth.

When term began, he realized with dismay that most classmates came from affluent families, well-versed in Western ways. They socialized in tight-knit urban circles while he stood shyly apart, unable to join their pop culture discussions.

In lectures, elegant terminology bandied casually by others left Rajesh bewildered. Catching the pitying looks classmates shot his worn notebook and trouser patches, he wanted to disappear into the earth.

Could someone from his humble beginnings ever fit into this sophisticated milieu? As days passed in confused isolation, Rajesh began doubting if he truly deserved this coveted university place after all., Feeling adrift, Rajesh wandered campus after orientation, lonely amid excited greetings filling the quad. Hailing from a place no one knew, he had no family or community here like city dwellers did.

Lost in thought, he hardly watched where he walked until colliding into a tall boy. Oh, I'm so sorry! said the other, dusting him off with concern. Are you alright?

Rajesh nodded mutely, cheeks burning at the attention. Noticing his distress, the boy smiled gently. I'm Dev. Freshman too. Want me to show you around?

Grateful for the unexpected kindness, Rajesh accepted. As Dev chattered easily, pointing out landmarks, Rajesh began to relax. Perhaps his isolation wouldn't last forever if he could find others like Dev - ones willing to see past differences to the person within.

That night, writing home, Rajesh spoke not of fears but promises - that through diligence and openness, he'd find his place here however challenging the path ahead seemed now. With Dev's welcome company and the support of his beloved village urging him on, Rajesh felt ready to take his first steps into an exciting future., Thank you for sharing this fascinating story outline. I have done my best to follow the beats provided for Chapter 2 and craft a cohesive narrative progression. This wraps up the beats specified for this chapter. Please let me know if you would like me to continue exploring additional parts of the story. I'm enjoying delving into Rajesh's journey and helping bring this tale to life.

# CHAPTER THREE

# A New World

Rajesh poured over his textbooks, but the equations and formulas swam before his eyes. In his village school, he had outpaced all his peers, grasping advanced mathematics with ease. But here at the university, hailing from an unknown village, he struggled to keep up.

In his first calculus class, the lecturer raced through derivatives and integrals, assuming a basic foundation Rajesh lacked. He frantically copied notes, but more words blurred together on the page. When examples were worked on the board, he stared blankly, unable to follow the steps.

At teatime, the other students excitedly discussed homework problems they had solved with little effort. Rajesh listened with a sinking heart, realizing how far behind he was. Only Dev, his roommate, noticed his apprehension.

"It's an adjustment for everyone," Dev said kindly. "The material moves fast, but you're clever - with practice, it will click."

But no matter how late Rajesh worked into the night,

formulas refused to stick in his tired brain. Finally throwing down his pencil in frustration, tears stung his eyes. What was he doing so far from home, failing so miserably among these city scholars?

The next morning, Dev suggested a study group. "We'll work through problems together step-by-step. Two minds are better than one." To Rajesh's surprise, Dev's patient explanations finally brought order to the chaos on the page. By their second session, he grasped the techniques. With Dev's guidance and encouragement, Rajesh began to believe in himself once more. In the next calculus lecture, as integrals danced across the board faster than ever, Rajesh focused intently. The professor presented an unusually difficult example involving nested integrals. He sighed, saying even the top students might struggle.

Rajesh's pencil hovered, following each step in his head. Others frantically scribbled while he paused, visualizing the solution. Then, a flash of insight came. Delicately balancing the integrals with a deft substitution, the solution blossomed before him. His pencil flew across the page.

A gasp rose from his classmates, still wrestling the problem. The professor stopped mid-explanation and turned. Rajesh stood calmly, worksheet outstretched. Mirrored in the board's integrals was his solution. Impressive, the professor said, examining Rajesh's work. Where did you study previously, that you grasp such concepts so naturally?

His peers turned to Rajesh in a new light as he explained his rural village roots. Thanks to Dev's guidance, and his own hard work bridging deficiencies, what was invisible to him now shone clear - and in that moment, Rajesh knew he belonged among these scholars after all. Rajesh immersed himself in mathematics, finding solace in its clarity and order. While other subjects evaded him, when he glimpsed mathematical concepts, they seemed to unfold before his eyes like beautiful glimpses of truth.

As exams began, Rajesh effortlessly solved complex calculus and algebra questions far beyond his peers. He finished early, double-checking intricately balanced equations and integrals with care. Elsewhere though, memorizing historical dates or analyzing dense poems gave him headache.

Nonetheless, when results posted, Rajesh had topped both calculus and algebra exams. His mathematics professors, already impressed by class contributions, commended his natural talent and work ethic. But other marks, while passable, reminded him of lurking deficits from his village roots that mathematics alone could not overcome.

Dev, ever supportive, said grades were not the goal. You will achieve so much Rajesh, by following your gifts and intuition. Stay determined and your talents will shine through. Heartened, Rajesh resolved to balance dedication in mathematics with diligent self-study in weaker areas. With Dev's friendship and his own resilient spirit, he would continually grow., With a sigh, Rajesh dropped his history textbook, rubbing tired eyes. His roommate Dev looked up from similar struggles. "It seems some subjects were not meant for us country folk," Dev said with a smile.

Rajesh laughed, grateful for Dev's humor. Though from

another village, Dev faced the same culture shocks as Rajesh adjusting to city life and university rigor. Yet where Rajesh floundered, Dev smoothly grasped foreign concepts. Despite humble origins, Dev's mathematics acumen rivaled the best scholars. Lecturers praised his solutions' innovation and clarity.

"How do you find problems so intriguing while I struggle even with basics?" Rajesh asked one night. Dev replied that as a child, solving puzzles sparked joy that steered him towards mathematics. Now, it calmed his mind like contemplation. Though peers mocked their roots, Dev believed education could uplift villages, giving rural youth wings. His patience teaching Rajesh reflected this compassion. Finding kinship and guidance in Dev, Rajesh's self-doubt lessened as together, they explored the elegance of numbers. During late-night study sessions, Dev decoded algebraic conundrums by lamplight while Rajesh watched, enraptured. With infinite patience, Dev walked him through each step, relating abstractions to concrete examples. As concepts once hazy sharpened into focus, Rajesh needed less guidance. Soon, he filled gaps in Dev's own understanding, their exchange flowering into collaboration.

Over steaming chai breaks, easy conversation replaced earlier silence. Rajesh shared village memories which elicited Dev's in kind. Laughter punctuated revelations of shared rural quirks, finding solace in such bonds of familiarity within urban unfamiliarity. Appreciating Dev's empathy that validated his struggles, Rajesh's doubts receded. With renewed dedication honed by Dev's wisdom, equations long insoluble now unravelled.

Where once lost amid lecture complexity, Rajesh now formulated innovative problems. Witnessing his comprehension blossom sparked Dev's joy as much as Rajesh's own. 'See how far you've come!' Dev beamed after a breakthrough, pride in Rajesh's redemption kindling belief in each other's potential. Gratitude and camaraderie planting seeds for a fellowship to withstand future challenges. Thus nurtured, Rajesh's talents took root and flourished. One rainy evening, as Dev transcribed equations at a frenzied pace, Rajesh's concentration faltered. Outside, the city hustle had dimmed into a bleak drone, heightening his loneliness. "Sometimes I feel I don't belong here," he confessed softly.

Dev looked up with understanding. "The city seems designed against us outsiders. But know that you have value, regardless what these privileged think." He told then of missing his own village, green fields instead of grey. How at first, loneliness keened sharper than homesickness. Dev had shut himself away, fearing exposure as an outsider fraud.

This admission surprised Rajesh - Dev, ever patient and bright, suffered too? Seeing his vulnerability bolstered Rajesh's courage. "Your friendship lightens theload. It gives me strength knowing we face this together." Dev squeezed his hand in wordless gratitude for the solace of solidarity. A bond began to bloom that night between the two scholars, roots digging deeper than any temporary loneliness could disturb as together they made the city theirs. Rajesh and Dev found shared understanding reassured where individual worries might overwhelm. Knowing another walked the same path lessened loneliness' sting. During stressful periods—exams, rejection letters—they buoyed each other's spirits.

"We'll study through the night if we must!" Dev vowed once when complex equations proved barricades against sleep. Their steady encouragement where self-doubt crept in fortified failing resolve.

After a calculus marks downgrade left Rajesh disheartened, Dev listened patiently then said, "Let anger fuel progress, not self-reproach. Together we'll ensure next time you earn your rightful place."

When Dev grew ill with fever, Rajesh ensured soup and textbooks within reach. "Rest, my friend. On recovery, I'll explain all you've missed."

Bonding through difficulties deepened their fellowship beyond superficial friendship. Each instance of support sowed understanding and trust that would endure adversity. Though homesick at times alone, together they found belonging—a found family more soothing than distant relatives. United against the challenges of academy and assimilation, their partnership thrived. Dear Mother,

Your last letter brought me joy, filling my days with memories of home. I hope this finds you in good health and spirits, tending your roses as the monsoon arrives.

My university life continues apace. Studies tax both body and soul at times, yet perseverance grants slow rewards. Of great solace remains Dev - his friendship lightens any load, as through shared struggles we find strength. Knowing another walks the same path lessens feeling an outsider. Our bond has become most precious.

While I miss Panchpota's familiarity, Dev's wise counsel eases city life's assimilation. With encouragement along frustrations, he kindles possibility in problems and bolsters flagging courage. Such empathy and care were providence's gift for this transition.

I think too of your sacrifice enabling my pursuit here. Though the road proved steeper than expected, your belief in me was shelter in darkest storms. With Dev beside, your love across distances lifts my heart higher than any loneliness might weigh it down.

My blessings and all my success I will dedicate to rewarding your faith. Please give my thanks to Brother and blessings to Father and sisters. I remain, your most grateful son.
Yours always,
Rajesh

# CHAPTER FOUR

# Rising Tides of Talent and Friendship

The morning of his second-year calculus exam, Rajesh sat jittery at his desk as he reviewed formulas and theorems one final time. He had been practicing problems relentlessly for weeks with Dev's help, pushing past lingering doubts to prepare thoroughly. When the exam papers were distributed, Rajesh took a deep breath and dived in, working through each question with calm concentration.

Hours later, as he emerged from the exam hall feeling confident in his responses, Rajesh was surprised by how naturally the concepts flowed from his mind onto the page. The frantic cramming of past exams seemed needless now; through regular study, the subject had truly become clearer. That evening, celebrating at their usual tea stall with Dev, Rajesh's suspicions were confirmed - he had received full marks, excelling all others in his class. Word began to spread of the gifted village boy who solved complex integrals with ease. For the first time, Rajesh allowed himself to feel pride in his accomplishments, rather than dismissing them as mere good fortune. His growing mastery of the subject was undeniable, encouraging greater faith in his abilities and place at the university. Though challenges remained, Rajesh felt surer than ever that with perseverance and the support of friends, he could achieve all he endeavored... That same week, the university's mathematics department convened for their monthly faculty meeting. As exam results were reviewed, Professor Varma spoke up in surprise. "It seems we have a remarkable student in our midst - this Rajesh fellow from rural Bengal has scored a perfect hundred percent in calculus yet again. His intuitions for complex problems are unmatched amongst even our postgraduates. I've asked him to assist me with research and he displays a natural gift I've not encountered before."

The others nodded, sharing their impressions of Rajesh's brilliant yet humble character. "He stays back after every lecture to better understand even the most advanced topics," remarked Professor Sinha. "And gets them all while continuing to tutor less fortunate peers without complaint. It's no exaggeration to say Rajesh's skills in mathematics dwarf all others of his year," agreed Professor Malhotra.

As the discussion turned to selecting candidates for the upcoming international student exchange program, Professor Varma recommended Rajesh without hesitation. "This opportunity could expose his gifts to the world. With proper nurturing and challenge, who knows how far Rajesh might go?" The faculty voted unanimously to put Rajesh forward, curious to see if the village boy truly held the potential to reshape the frontiers of his field... Moments later, Rajesh was summoned to the Dean's office, perplexed by this sudden meeting. The Dean smiled warmly. Thanks to your exceptional skills, we'd like to accelerate your studies, Rajesh. Normally a junior-level course, we're granting you entry into Advanced Calculus this semester itself.

Rajesh was stunned. But Sir, I'm only a sophomore. The Dean waved this off. Rules are made to be bent for exceptional talent. You'll also be our nominee for the international exchange program in Germany next winter. We feel this exposure could hugely benefit your development.

Rajesh could barely process this rapid change in fortune. His professors believed in him so wholly? He thanked the Dean profusely even as doubts lingered. Could he truly handle such advanced material so soon? But looking to his future, how could he refuse this kind of opportunity? That evening, Rajesh shared the news with Dev over a jubilant dinner, wonder and gratitude filling his heart. With his friend's faith and the university's endorsement, Rajesh pledged to make the very most of the chance bestowed on him through diligent study. Little did he know how profoundly the coming year would reshape his life's path in unexpected ways..., Rajesh began tackling Advanced Calculus with his usual focus but noticed sideways glances and whispering in the corridors. Word had spread of the village boy excelling far beyond his years. One day, a fellow student confrontationally demanded to know Rajesh's "secret".

Remaining calm, Rajesh replied "I have only studied diligently with the guidance of respected professors. There is no secret - only commitment to learning."

Later, Dev warned of growing resentment from peers unable to match Rajesh's natural gifts and success despite his humble origins. But Rajesh shrugged off such petty jealousies.

"Let them think what they will. I am here only to learn, not compete," he told Dev sincerely. When the Dean privately asked if jealousy was affecting Rajesh, he assured, "My priority lies in gaining knowledge, not status or prestige. As long as respected faculty support my learning, peers' opinions matter little."

His earnest manner disarmed growing critics. Rajesh kept his head down in his studies, deflecting attention to help others understand complex topics. Through patience and integrity, resentment slowly faded as his character emerged. Rajesh cared not for empty rivalry, but only for unlocking mathematics' depths through diligence and intuition. While others partied weekends away, Rajesh could often be found immersed amongst towering shelves of the university library. Here he delved into advanced theorems and complex equations, chasing mathematical understandings beyond his years with single-minded dedication.

On nights when even dedicated peers grew weary, Rajesh remained at his table, formulas swirling through his mind as the outside world faded. Dev sometimes joined, helping clarify subtle concepts before retiring to rest. But Rajesh pushed on, engrossed by the subject's intuitive beauty and determined to push his skills even further.

When dawn light filtered through high-arched windows, only then would Rajesh gather his notes to snatch some hours of sleep. Yet even dreams held mathematical musings as subconsciously crafted solutions. Renewed, he would return to texts, refining intuitions with each reading.

Through such focused pursuits, what had once challenged Rajesh now seemed increasingly clear. His talents blossomed rapidly beyond classmates, gaining the respect of esteemed professors. But Rajesh cared not for praise or prestige, only perfecting his craft through diligence and study far into each night. For him, mathematics offered solace and purpose that superseded all else., One evening as spring exams neared, Rajesh found Dev brooding alone in their dorm room. My friend, what troubles you? he asked gently.

Dev sighed. No matter how much I study, your intuitions in math far surpass mine, Rajesh. Perhaps I do not belong at this university after all.

Rajesh sat close. Do not say such things. You remain the most gifted mathematician in our year aside from me. Where I see patterns, you see proofs - our talents simply differ in form.

He recounted how Dev's patient explanations first unlocked concepts for him, insisting Dev's friendship and guidance proved far more valuable than any exam score. You are not here to surpass Rajesh or others but to better understand this beautiful subject through diligent study. Have faith in the scholar that you are, as I have always had in you.

His words lifted Dev's down cast eyes. You ever reminded me why our bond proves the most precious aspect of this place, Rajesh. With your conviction in my abilities, how can I not believe in myself once more? Youtruly are the best of friends., With smiling eyes, Rajesh clasped Dev's shoulder, glad to ease the self-doubt of one as deserving and integral to his success as the one before him. Their bond of empathy and trust remained the firmest anchor through all challenges. Rajesh met Dev's eyes with a gentle smile. "True success isn't measured by prizes or prestige, my friend. It lies in constantly challenging ourselves to grow in knowledge and character. Awards may come and go, but the lessons we learn here will shape our lives forever."

He gazed out at the setting sun, thinking of countless discussions that had deepened his understanding. "Each new idea I grasp, each way I can help another - these bring me far greater joy than any exam score. What matters is bettering ourselves through diligent study. The rest will follow in due time."

Dev pondered his words. "You ever remind me of what truly drives my passion for mathematics. It's not marks or rank, but solving problems that seemed impossible. Pushing past what I knew yesterday."

"Exactly." Rajesh beamed. "As long as our focus lies in continuous self-improvement, success will take care of itself. Don't lose sight of your gifts, Dev. With persistence and each other's support, there's no limit to what we may achieve."

His friend's steady reassurance lifted Dev's spirits once more. Their bond proved the true reward of this journey, guiding both toward fulfilling destinies through steadfast commitment to growing in knowledge and character. That evening, Rajesh sat writing a letter by lamplight.

Dear Amma and others,

My studies progress well and professors assure a bright future. But I wish to always remember - this success is due to your sacrifices and the seed Professor Rao sowed all those years ago in our village. His lessons first sparked my love of learning. Your support then allowed that spark to blossom.

Now as I navigate new horizons, Dev remains a brother guiding my every step. Through empathy and intellect, he proves the true gift of this journey. Each challenge we overcome together only strengthens our bond and skills.

Know that wherever this path may lead, a part of my heart will always belong to Panchpota. I strive to make both our village and this university proud through diligence, discipline and service to others. Your blessings carry me forward and will forever shape who I become.

With deepest gratitude and love,
Rajesh

Folding the letter, Rajesh smiled thinking of familiar faces. While horizons broadened each day, his commitment to values learned as a village boy would stay steadfast. With

each new lesson, he felt truer to the scholar and man
Professor Rao and his family had nurtured him to be.

# Navigating New Horizons

Rajesh walked out of the exam hall with a lightness in his step. All those hours of late-night study sessions with Dev had paid off. He knew he had aced the calculus exam, answering even the most complex problems with ease.

News of his performance spread quickly through the mathematics department. Professor Varma congratulated Rajesh, telling him he had displayed a rare gift. It seemed all of Rajesh's hard work was being recognized.

A few days later, Rajesh received a summons to the Dean's office. When he arrived, he found Professor Varma already there along with the Dean. "Please have a seat, Rajesh," the Dean said kindly. "Professor Varma has nominated you for an exceptional opportunity and we think you are most deserving."

Rajesh's mind began racing as the Dean explained. Thanks to his outstanding exam results, Rajesh would be allowed to take Advanced Calculus early, as a sophomore. But there was more - Professor Varma had suggested Rajesh as the university's nominee for their prestigious international student exchange program in Germany.

Germany? Rajesh could hardly believe it. An opportunity to study abroad had seemed like a distant dream. "We feel this exchange will help elevate your gifts to a higher level," Professor Varma said. "What do you say, will you accept?"

Still in a state of shock and delight, Rajesh could only nod. He was accepting more than just this exchange - he was embracing all the possibilities now open before him, thanks to the faith and support of his mentors. Rajesh was determined to make the most of this chance and represent his university well on the world stage. Here is a continuation of Chapter 5:

Rajesh could barely contain his joy as he thanked the Dean and Professor Varma. He rushed to share the news with Dev, who was just as thrilled for his friend. "Germany!" Dev exclaimed. "This is an amazing opportunity. You simply must go."

In the ensuing weeks, Rajesh prepared diligently for his trip. He researched the university in Munich where he would be studying and familiarized himself with the German language and culture. Every chance he got, Rajesh reviewed his calculus notes, determined to represent his abilities at the highest level.

Soon the departure date arrived. Rajesh said goodbye to his mother and family, proud that he could make them proud through this achievement. At the airport, Dev wished him the best. "Have the time of your life and soak up all the knowledge you can. I expect detailed letters about your adventures!"

As Rajesh settled into his seat and the plane took flight, he gazed out the window in awe. A whole new world was about to unfold before him. Though nervous, Rajesh was filled with eager anticipation for this opportunity to experience international academia and broaden his perspectives. He had a feeling this exchange would prove transformational in the best ways possible. Here is a continuation of Chapter 5:

That evening, Rajesh sat down to write a letter to his family back in India.

Dear Mother, Didi and Bhaiya,

I hope this letter finds you all well. I am writing to share some exciting news - I have been selected for a student exchange program in Germany! Can you believe it, I will be studying at a university abroad for a semester. All of my hard work and your sacrifices seem to be paying off.

I know leaving home again was not easy, but your support means the world to me. This opportunity would not be possible without the foundation of learning you provided. The values you taught me of discipline, kindness and faith are sustaining me even thousands of miles from home.

Please pass on my thanks to Professor Rao and the whole village for their continued blessings. I think of Panchpota each day and hope to make you all proud with my conduct here. Rest assured that wherever this path may lead, my heart remains in our little corner of Bengal.

Give everyone my love and prayers for health and happiness. I hope to be home again soon to share more of my adventures. Until then, know that your son is living his dreams through your strength and belief in him.

With love and gratitude,
Rajesh

He smiled, hoping the letter would bring a joyful glow to their day, as news of this blessing had for him. His family's love kept him rooted as new horizons continually opened. Here is a continuation of Chapter 5:

In the weeks leading up to his departure, Rajesh spent many evenings with Dev researching the university in Munich where he would be studying. They pored over maps of the city, noting landmarks and transportation routes. Rajesh practiced basic German phrases, though the guttural sounds were strange to his ears.

"It's exciting to think of all the cultural experiences awaiting you," Dev remarked. But beneath his excited tone, Rajesh detected a trace of sadness at their impending separation.

Dev's support over the past two years had been invaluable. Rajesh was anxious about navigating a foreign academic system without his friend's guidance. "Promise you'll write often with all the latest gossip from lectures," he said lightly, though there was an underlying plea in his voice.

"And you must do the same - describe every adventure in detail!" Dev replied. But they both knew distance and new circumstances could so easily alter friendships. An unspoken worry lurked beneath their eager conversations and plans to keep in touch regularly.

On the evening before his flight, Rajesh and Dev stayed up late reminiscing about their time at university together so far. Rajesh tried to quell his swirling nerves, focusing on this opportunity to further his education. But he knew in a foreign land, amid unfamiliar challenges, he would miss his anchor - his dear friend Dev. Here is a continuation of Chapter 5:

The days rushed by in a flurry of frenzied packing as Rajesh and Dev prepared for their respective journeys. They double checked travel documents, packed clothing suitable for varying seasons, medical supplies, power adapters.

On his last night in the dorm, Rajesh meticulously repacked his bag twice, fussing over every small item. What if I've forgotten something essential? he fretted. Dev forced him to sit, calming his nerves with tales from classic adventures.

See this as an opportunity for exploration, not worry, my friend. You've faced far worse obstacles with perseverance. Embrace each unexpected encounter - who knows what gifts may come?

Rajesh knew Dev spoke wisdom, yet unease gnawed within. What challenges would a foreign land hold? New cultures, languages, people, customs - it was too vast to fathom.

That night, conversation drifted to speculations of the unknown ahead. Would the exchange deepen Rajesh's knowledge or lead him elsewhere? What wonders might Dev find in America?

As darkness fell, an anticipatory hush settled over them. Two kindred souls, embarking on journeys that could spin them far from this bond. Come what may, this friendship would endure, anchoring their spirits through any storms., Here is a continuation of Chapter 5:

All too soon, the morning of departure arrived. At the airport, Dev embraced Rajesh tightly. Go well, my brother. Make our country proud.

Rajesh's insides twisted as he nodded, unable to speak past the knot in his throat. He turned toward the departure gate, stopping to glance back at Dev one last time. His friend waved with an encouraging smile.

As Rajesh settled into his seat, nerves jangled within like an unstrung veil. He gazed out the window at the bustling tarmac, awash in activity yet feeling solitary amid the crowds. Would this plane deliver him to new opportunities or uncertainties?

The roar of engines pulled his mind back with a jolt as the aircraft accelerated down the runway. Higher and higher they climbed through the clouds, leaving familiar landscapes smaller below. A vast expanse of unknown stretched vast ahead, filled with untold possibilities.

Rajesh dug out his notebook, hoping to distill turbulent

thoughts onto the page. But as equations danced before his eyes, so too did visions of all that may await - knowledge, experiences, people and places beyond imagination. He was soaring to a transformed world; whether for good or ill, only discovery would reveal. Here is a continuation of Chapter 5:

As the plane leveled off on its westward trajectory, Rajesh gazed down at the patchwork of fields dotting the land below. Thoughts turned inevitably to those far away, continuing lives he had left behind.

He wondered if his mother was overseeing farm duties in their village, surrounded by familiar sights and sounds. If Dev's family was working in their paddy fields under the heat of the noon sun. If children were playing along the riverbank, splashing and laughing without a care.

How distant and small his simple childhood world seemed from this vantage, and yet it remained stitched into his being. Rajesh recalled walking those dusty lanes, stopping to marvel at peculiar insects or mathematical puzzles woven into daily tasks.

Though excited for new adventures ahead, part of Rajesh's heart would always dwell in his small corner of Bengal. There, he had discovered his calling and been nourished with love, roots from which his dreams took wing. As clouds obscured the patchwork below, Rajesh gave silent thanks for the blessings and strength of his family keeping him aloft., Here is a continuation of Chapter 5:

After a long flight, Rajesh felt groggy yet restless as the

plane touched down in Munich. The unfamiliar syllables drifting over the airport tannoy sounded like an alien tongue.

Stepping onto the jetway, a rush of chill air awakened his senses. Rajesh gazed out the window at a landscape blanketed in white, devoid of the vibrant colors that defined home. Everything was muted under a pewter sky.

In the terminal, signage and announcements flew by in an incomprehensible blur. Rajesh clutched his passport like a talisman, feeling very small amid bustling crowds. How would he find his bearing in this foreign city alone?

As he exited the building, the cold hit like a wall. Rajesh shivered, pulling his jacket tight and squinting against fat flakes drifting lazily down. This was no longer India - the rules of his world had been reconfigured without warning.

Hailing a cab with hesitant German, Rajesh surreptitiously pinched his arm. No, this was real - a transformative chapter had begun in a land beyond imagination. Though nerves danced, Rajesh was filled with determination to make the most of this chance to grow.

# CHAPTER SIX

# A Semester Abroad

Rajesh stepped onto the busy streets of Munich, overwhelmed by the bustling crowds and foreign sounds. Tall buildings loomed all around and signs were printed in an unfamiliar script. He lugged his heavy suitcase, uncertain of which direction led to the university campus. Just then, a gentle voice called out "Do you need help finding your way?" He turned to see a smiling blond woman gazing at him inquisitively. "I'm Leah. Are you one of the exchange students from India?" she asked. Rajesh nodded gratefully. Leah's cheerful manner instantly put him at ease.

She offered to show him to the campus, engaging Rajesh in friendly chatter as they walked. Leah expressed excitement about meeting students from abroad and hoped they could become good friends. Rajesh was surprised by her welcoming demeanor, so different from the reactions he sometimes faced in India. A feeling of lightness filled his heart, buoyed by Leah's kindness on his first lonely day in an unfamiliar land.

By the time they reached the gates, Rajesh's nerves had settled. Leah gave him a tour of the grounds, pointing out important buildings and helping him find his dormitory.

They exchanged numbers so Leah could introduce Rajesh to others. As she walked away waving, Rajesh stood gazing after her smiling face, thinking maybe this foreign adventure wouldn't be so hard with people like Leah by his side. For the first time, he felt a glimmer of hope for the semester ahead. Rajesh entered the large lecture hall, scanning the sea of unfamiliar faces for an open seat. Just then, a cheerful wave caught his eye. It was Leah, beckoning him over to the spot beside her.

"Good morning! I'm glad we have this class together," she said warmly as Rajesh sat down. Her kind smile instantly lifted his nerves. Leah introduced him to the students nearby, who greeted Rajesh politely though with less enthusiasm.

As the professor began speaking, Leah noticed Rajesh's focused expression and tapped notes to him on the intricacies of organic chemistry. She possessed both intelligence and patience, explaining concepts clearly without condescension. During the break, she inquired about India with genuine curiosity. Rajesh found himself relaxing in Leah's cheerful company, her interest in his culture helping him feel more at ease in this foreign place. Perhaps with good-natured friends like Leah, his exchange semester might turn out to be quite agreeable after all. Rajesh found himself looking forward to his classes just to spend time with Leah. Her bright presence illuminated the dreary lecture halls, and she had a way of making even the most complex topics delightfully understandable. Between classes, they would often linger chatting animatedly about their studies and beyond.

Rajesh was surprised to find Leah as intellectually curious about various fields as she was skilled in her own chemistry domain. She listened with rapt attention as he described pioneering Indian mathematicians and the philosophical traditions behind different calculation methods. In turn, Leah introduced Rajesh to new scientific discoveries and theories with infectious enthusiasm.

During lively debates on their walks across campus, Rajesh came to appreciate Leah's insightful yet thoughtful analyses. Rather than arrogant assertions, she qualified hypotheses and maintained an open, inquisitive mind. Her intellect was as warm and welcoming as her smile.

While other students focused on socializing, Rajesh and Leah found solace in each other's company as kindred spirits united by their passion for knowledge. Unconsciously, they began seeking each other out, their daily interactions becoming the most memorable parts of each day. Perhaps, Rajesh thought, he had gained more than just an insightful classmate - he had found a true friend. One evening as they walked out of the chemistry lab, Rajesh noticed the sun had already set. He was surprised to find that he and Leah had whiled away the afternoon debating energetically without noticing the time.

"It seems we've missed dinner," Leah laughed. "Would you like to grab a bite with me instead?" delight flooded Rajesh at the prospect of extending their conversation. They found a cozy cafe still serving snacks and settled in with steaming cups of tea.

As they chatted easily about everything from molecule

configurations to Leah's childhood home, the atmosphere felt intimate and warm despite the nighttime chill outside. Leah possessed an easy smile and playful wit that brought out Rajesh's rarely-seen playful side. Laughter came more freely to him in her cheerful company, relieving him of self-consciousness.

The sky darkened as their conversation flowed unhindered. Only when Rajesh's yawns could no longer be suppressed did they reluctantly part ways, exchanging wistful smiles at the prospect of another stimulating day together tomorrow. As he drifted off to sleep, Rajesh replayed their lively discussion and realized with surprise that he had quite forgotten this was only their second meeting. A fast friendship seemed to be blooming between them. The next day, as Rajesh browsed the dining hall alone, an eager voice called him over. "Rajesh, come eat with us!" said Leah, who waved from a table full of chatty students.

He hesitated, intimidated by the crowd. But Leah smiled warmly. "Don't be shy. Everyone's dying to meet you." Her disarming manner set him at ease.

Leah did the introductions, her peers responding with friendly curiosity about India which eased Rajesh's nerves. The food and flowing conversation distracted from his self-consciousness.

During a lull, a boisterous male student launched into a spirited debate with Leah. Rajesh watched, impressed by her wit and sunny demeanor that defused tensions. At the next opportunity, Leah drew Rajesh into the discussion with a gentle prompt.

To his surprise, Rajesh found himself articulating viewpoints clearly. Laughter and encouragement met his contributions, Leah beaming proudly at his side. As the group parted ways, many bade Rajesh a warm farewell. He smiled, buoyed by Leah's kindness in ensuring he felt an accepted part of things. Her warmth was slowly melting away his foreign aloofness., Rajesh gazed at the spread in the cafeteria in wonder. Colorful snacks crowded every shelf, their textures and aromas, unlike anything in India. "What is all this?" he asked Leah.

She smiled. "Let me introduce you! This cheese is soft and creamy, baked into twists. And these sausages are grilled until crispy." Leah encouraged him to sample each with obvious relish.

Rajesh took tentative bites, surprised by subtle yet rich flavors he had never encountered. Leah watched eagerly as comprehension dawned on his face. "Delicious, isn't it? You simply must try our strudel next - flaky pastry filled with sweet apples."

At her suggestion, Rajesh savored the buttery crust melting on his tongue. A sigh of pleasure escaped him, and Leah laughed. "I'm so glad you're enjoying local specialties. There's a whole world of tastes to explore here!"

Her enthusiasm was contagious. Rajesh began pointing to foods with inquisitive eyes, and Leah obliged each request with warmth. As they compared flavors to Indian cuisine, Rajesh realized with gratitude how Leah shone light upon this new landscape, making the unfamiliar feel welcome through her guidance. That weekend, Leah showed Rajesh around Munich. She chattered knowledgeably about landmarks, weaving in cultural context. At a bustling square, she noted similarities to Indian bazaars yet differences in goods sold.

By a crystal lake, she asked Rajesh to describe India's varied geography. As he spoke of terrain unfamiliar to her, Leah hung on every captivating word. Later, over coffee and strudel, their discussion turned philosophical.

Leah listened with care as Rajesh expressed hopes for his nation's future, noting parallels in Germany's difficult past. Rather than disagreements, they found shared beliefs in equality and justice. Her thoughtful questions conveyed openness, not judgment, helping Rajesh feel understood.

That evening, they strolled a quiet street at twilight. Lantern light glowed warmly through cafe windows as couples passed, arm in arm. Leah's presence seemed to enrich even sights familiar to her. Engrossed in lively debate beneath a painted sky, Rajesh felt his world expand through her insight and empathy. A newfound closeness blossomed between them through such culturally bridging talks. As their steps slowed, smiles were exchanged with reluctance to end the illuminating day. My dear Dev,

I hope this letter finds you well. My days in Germany are passing in a joyful blur thanks to the new friend I've made - Leah, a bright chemistry student. From the moment she showed me around campus on my first day, her cheerful manner has put me at ease.

In class and during breaks, Leah is full of insightful questions that ignite my mind. Our debates range widely yet always feel stimulating. She listens with care to tales of India and makes even complex topics understandable through patience and skill. Leah has ensured I am comfortable among her lively friend group too.

Beyond studies, Leah is introducing me to Munich – its flavors, sights, and history. Our walks are filled with thoughtful discussions bridging cultures. Leah's empathy and openness help me feel truly understood, and she makes even familiar places new through insight.

I cannot recall the last time I laughed as much or looked so forward to each day. Leah has melted away my feelings of foreignness with her warm companionship. Please thank our professors for granting me this experience, and know that I am making the most of each moment, thinking of you both often. Until next we meet, your friend, Rajesh. There are no more beats provided for Chapter 6 in the reference material. The chapter appears to be completed based on the beats and details given. Unless additional narrative direction is provided, I do not have any new content to add at this time.

# CHAPTER SEVEN

# Blossoming Romance

As the weeks passed, Rajesh found himself looking forward to his daily meetings with Leah more than anything else. While their conversations initially centered around class topics and cultural exchanges, they had begun delving deeper into each other's lives, dreams, and perspectives.

One sunny afternoon, as they strolled through the University botanical gardens debating philosophical ideas, Rajesh was struck by the sparkle in Leah's eyes and the enthusiasm with which she discussed concepts. A flutter arose in his heart as he realized her kindred spirit and passion matched his own.

That evening, Rajesh noticed the first fallen leaves of autumn drift past as he gazed out of his window, lost in thought. Leah's beaming face floated before him, replaying their day's discussions and moments of shared laughter. A sense of calm welled within Rajesh, unlike anything he had known before.

The next day, with a bouquet of dahlias in hand, Rajesh sought out Leah after class, hoping to extend their time together. On seeing him, Leah broke into a smile brighter than the sun. As they walked, Rajesh offered her the flowers with a shy admiration. Leah accepted them gently, touched them.

In the cozy cafe they frequented, over steaming cups of coffee, Rajesh and Leah spoke of life's profound yet simple beauty. They found solace in each other's company, an unspoken affinity nourishing their blossoming affection. Both vowed silently to nurture this kindred bond on Rajesh's return to India, come what may. As the leaves turned vibrant shades of orange and red around them, Rajesh and Leah continued their daily walks through the quiet university grounds. One afternoon, as they strolled alongside the gurgling brook, Leah remarked on the fleeting nature of beauty in the natural world.

Rajesh found himself gazing not at the landscape, but at Leah's profile, admiring the keen intelligence shining behind her eyes. In that moment, he was struck by an epiphany - it was not just Leah's looks or lively spirit that drew him, but the rare kindness and empathy within her gentle soul. Few had shown him such unwavering acceptance and understanding.

That evening, as they parted ways at Leah's doorstep, Rajesh hesitated, words escaping him. Leah spared him, smiling knowingly. She grasped his hands in hers and insisted he share all that weighed on his mind, for she wished only to lighten his load, never cause more burden. Her selfless reassurance moved Rajesh deeply.

In Leah's compassionate gaze and quiet strength, Rajesh found an anchor, strengthening his resolve to make the most of this precious time together. A warmth grew in his heart for this dear friend, whose shining perseverance in their discussions never ceased awakening his mind to new horizons. One sunny weekend, as they strolled the university grounds discussing an upcoming exam, Leah shyly proposed a picnic by the flowing creek. Rajesh readily accepted his heart, swelling with joy.

The next day, laden with a woven basket filled with bread, fruits, and wine, they settled under a flowering dogwood tree. As a gentle breeze rustled petals upon the grass, Leah coaxed childhood memories from Rajesh of village fairs and adventures with his brother.

Rajesh regaled her in turn with tales of Leah's family farm, their animals, and joyous festivals. Leah's vibrant descriptions transported Rajesh, reminding him of simpler times. Here, under warm sun and blooms, distances seemed bridged by their bond.

As evening fell, the pair packed remnants of their meal slowly, unwilling for the day to end. Rajesh noticed a pink blossom nestled in Leah's honeyed locks, leaving it be. They lingered in each other's company, solace amid looming change. Both vowed silently to nurture the seed of affection growing between them on Rajesh's return home., As dusk fell, Rajesh and Leah strolled the winding path alongside the burbling creek once more. The setting sun cast the sky afire in hues of tangerine and rose. They paused by the footbridge to watch the light fade from the peaks in a blanket of violet.

A cooling breeze lifted whispered leaves and ruffled hair

tenderly. Turning to smile their gratitude for this moment, their eyes met and held - glimpsing reflections of kindred spirits within. Barely daring to breathe, Rajesh lifted a hand to gently cradle Leah's soft cheek. Leaning into his palm ever so slightly, she mirrored the gesture with her own.

As their fingers entwined, all else fell silent but for the hush of crickets and their hearts swelling in tandem. Lips met softly, eyes drifting shut as days' conversations culminated in this embrace. All that had drawn them together found voice without words - respect, care, and solace in each other's presence. The first blooms of affection took gentle root in the glow of twilight, nurtured by souls that had found safe harbor in the other. As dusk deepened to night along the winding bank, Rajesh and Leah lingered close in the moon's gentle light. Gazing softly into eyes that reflected her soul, Rajesh brushed stray locks from Leah's face and tucked them tenderly behind her ear.

Leah leaned into his caring touch, alight with a warmth unlike any other. Tilting her smiling face up to his, she closed her eyes, leaving all to the guiding hand of fate. Rajesh's heartbeat quickened at her trust, mirroring the blooms awakening within her nearness.

Lowering his lips to hers, their first kiss was a sigh - delicate yet profound. All that had drawn their wandering spirits together now spoke through this cherished union; respect, solace, and the promise of understanding beyond borders. Love unexpectedly answered their longings, blossoming where least expected in another's tender care.

As they drew apart, eyes luminous even in darkness, Rajesh

whispered her name like a prayer. Leah's answering smile held all the wonder and reassurance of dreams fulfilled against all belief. Hand in hand they walked back quietly, hearts bursting yet at peace, nourished by affection's first glimmer under a canopy of watching stars., As they strolled the moonlit paths, Rajesh walked Leah gently to her doorstep. Lingering outside, both reluctant to part yet their souls buzzing with newfound affection, Rajesh expressed gratitude for this day and her welcoming spirit that had eased his adjustment in a foreign land.

Leah squeezed his hands in return, insisting it was she who felt grateful for the meeting of like minds. With shy smiles and fingertips tracing tender cheekbones, they shared a final, fleeting kiss beneath whispering shadows. Reluctantly drawing away to let her rest, Rajesh whispered reassurances to carry in her heart till the morrow, his own full to bursting.

Waving softly as she disappeared into welcoming warmth, Rajesh stared up at a sky aglow with brilliant promise. Heart buoyed by pure affection's sustaining light, he began the tranquil walk back hoping to somehow capture this joy to share with his faraway friend Dev. Till then, sweet dreams of sunlight and blossoms would have to suffice. With Leah's smile to guide him, the roads ahead seemed bright indeed. Back in his dorm room lit by lamplight, Rajesh sat at his desk smiling softly. Taking up his pen, he began to pour out all that filled his heart to his dearest friend, knowing Dev would understand:

_My friend,_
_The evening brings joyous news - I have met someone

as rare and compassionate as your kind spirit. Leah is sunlight-given form, lighting my days with smiles and insights that nourish the soul._

_Where once I saw only duty in this journey, now purpose blossoms anew in her presence. With her, all barriers fade and worlds unite in shared wonder at life's fleeting beauty. I have seen glimpses of joy beyond imagining in her eyes and felt life's promise in her embrace under the stars._

_You alone know my wandering heart as it longs for home. Yet with Leah, distance falls away and I find safe harbor, as with you. I pray this bond transcends all partings, as ours has, to journey wherever our paths may lead._ _Till we meet again, my brother - may your sleep be light, as mine will be with her memory to buoy my dreams._

_All affection,
Rajesh_

Sealing the letter with a small smile, Rajesh blew out the lamp, heart full at love's sweet unfolding and the trusted friend who would celebrate this joy with him across seas. As the sun rose over a new day, Rajesh sought Leah out eager to walk with her among blooming orchards. Seeing him approach, Leah's smile lit the pathway like dawn.

Hand in hand they ambled softly through morning dew, sharing smiles and shy, fleeting kisses of newfound affection. As the cathedral bells chimed in the distance, they paused beneath a flowering bough entwined with promise.

Gazing into eyes that held hope and wonder alike, Rajesh spoke of returning home at the semester's end. But Leah silenced him with a lingering kiss, insisting their bond transcend all borders to journey with them lifelong wherever fate led.

"Distance can't diminish what's grown here in friendship and understanding's fertile soil. Our spirits are woven as these branches; kept alive by memory until paths cross again," she smiled.

Heart full, Rajesh nodded, breathing in her comfort one last time before reality called them forth once more. Stepping into daylight hand in hand, love's seeds had taken root to blossom in joy's timing, nourished by faith that brought them together under this sky.

# CHAPTER EIGHT

# A Promise Across Continents

The last days of Rajesh's semester in Germany flew by. Between attending fascinating lectures and exploring Munich's hidden treasures with Leah, he hardly noticed the winter turning to spring. All too soon, the closing ceremony arrived to mark the end of the exchange program.

As Rajesh helped pack his bags, a wave of sadness washed over him. In the few short months, this university campus had become as familiar as his own back home. He had learned so much both inside and outside the classroom - much of which he owed to his patient guide, Leah.

That evening, Rajesh and Leah strolled through the bustling platz one last time, taking in the sights and enjoying each other's company. The festive lights and sounds blurred around them as they spoke of everything and nothing, reluctant for this time together to end.

When they reached Leah's dormitory, Rajesh turned to her. "I cannot thank you enough for making this experience so meaningful. You have been my anchor in this new world."

Leah took both his hands in hers. "The pleasure was all mine. I am glad I could help shed some light on Germany for you." She paused, smiling shyly. "You must promise to keep in touch once you return home. Distance need not diminish what we have found here."

Rajesh returned the squeeze of her hands. "You have my word. I will write as soon as I arrive."

With smiles laced with sadness, they said their reluctant goodbyes. As Rajesh walked away, he clung to the hope that this new bond had only just begun. Here is the continuation of Chapter 8:

That week, each moment Rajesh and Leah spent together seemed brighter than the last. On their final picnic by the river, Rajesh found himself captivated, not just by Leah's insightful perspectives, but by the light in her eyes and her ready smile. There was a joyous spirit about her, even in the simplest of pleasures, that moved him.

As they watched the setting sun cast its golden glow on the rippling waters, Rajesh felt at peace. In Leah's company, he was reminded that even in foreign places, kindness could be found. She had shown him the beauty in differences through thoughtful discussions and little acts of care. More than anything, she had given solace to the loner she first met on campus.

Now, as the semester drew to its close, Rajesh felt her friendship had become his single greatest treasure from this experience abroad. A part of him yearned to stay near this kindred soul who understood his quiet nature and brought light to his days. But he knew they must soon say goodbye, and he would return to India with a full heart, carrying this gift wherever destiny took him next. Here is a continuation of Chapter 8 with the specified beat:

A few days before Rajesh's departure, Leah invited him on a picnic by the river. They packed a basket with bread, cheese and fruit from the market. As they strolled along the tree-lined path, pink and white blossoms floated lazily onto the rippling water.

When they found a grassy spot in the shade, Leah spread out a blanket. As they ate, she asked Rajesh about his childhood in India. He told her about exploring the forests near his village, climbing trees and catching frogs by the riverbank. Leah listened intently, visualizing the landscapes he described.

In return, Rajesh asked about Leah's early years. She spoke fondly of summer days spent picking berries with her siblings in the countryside. The warm sun and sweet fragrances flooding their senses as they played hide-and-seek between the bushes.

As Leah reminisced, Rajesh was struck by the similarities in their hearts despite the geographical distance between them. Both had found solace in nature, and treasured moments of togetherness with family. He was grateful to have glimpsed this side of her today, under the shade of blooming canopies like those from her memories. Their easy chat and shared laughs seemed to drift on the breeze, timeless as the flowing river before them. Here is a continuation of Chapter 8 focusing on Rajesh on the plane:

All too soon, Rajesh found himself gazing out the plane window as emerald forests and villages grew smaller below. His mind drifted back to golden memories of lazy summer afternoons with Leah.

He thought of their picnic by the flowing river, sharing laughter and snapshots of their lives under a blanket of pink blossoms. Quiet walks through the old town streets, lingering in bookshops and cafes to prolong each moment together.

Evenings spent stargazing from the bridge as the clock tower chimed in the distance, opening up about dreams and what truly mattered most. Leah's radiant smile, kind eyes and insightful spirit that lifted his own.

Now their time had come to an end, and Rajesh was returning to India with an unburdened heart. But deep within also lingered a promise - that their bond had only just begun, and distance would not dim the light she had brought into his life.

As pale blue faded into rose gold on the horizon, Rajesh watched the last shadows of summer cling to the waking earth below. He smiled, hoping that wherever her path may lead, Leah's spirit would continue bringing richness to all she met., Here is a continuation of Chapter 8 focusing on Rajesh's return home:

The familiar sounds and sights of Kolkata airport did little to lift Rajesh's heavy heart. As he rode home in a crowded bus, the chaotic streets felt muted after lively Munich.

Upon arriving in his village, Rajesh was greeted with enthusiasm by family and neighbors. Yet underneath the cheers and presents lay an emptiness none could fill. In Germany, every moment had bloomed with new discovery through Leah's guidance.

Now alone in his tiny room, the curtains drew him in like the closing of a chapter. He took Leah's last letter from his bag with a sigh, re-reading fond memories of adventures and inside jokes that now seemed far away.

In her stead, daily chores and solitary study loomed as a colorless routine. Rajesh wished he could still wander bookshops debating theories, or stroll gardens sharing easy laughter and deep talks under the stars. Leah's brightness had lit up his world, and without her, even home felt muted.

As first monsoon rains pattered the tin roof, Rajesh gazed at the letter once more, clutching its lingering warmth. He knew only time and their correspondence could mend this restless heart, until then, Germany would remain in his mind like the memory of a beautiful dream., Here is a continuation of Chapter 8 focusing on Rajesh's mother comforting him:

Rajesh's mother knew him better than most. As he gazed out at sheets of rain, she placed a gentle hand on his shoulder. My son, I see your spirits are heavy since returning. Change is never easy, but it brings growth too.

Rajesh looked into her kind eyes, shining with life's lessons. He found solace there as always. She spoke softly: Germany opened your world in wondrous ways, through adventures and friendship. Cherish each memory, but do not linger in old days. Leah would not want your light to dim.

New seasons come, as do fresh chances to blossom further. Your village also has things to offer - roots that ground you, and people who hold you dear. Joy can be found even in simple moments, if we open our eyes to see. The rains cannot last forever, my child, and your future awaits when skies are clear.

Rajesh embraced his mother gratefully. Her wisdom soothed restless thoughts like a balm. He knew in time, as other seeds were sown, his Germany experiences would remain poised to sprout again in moments of clarity and inspiration. For now, home's shelter would have to be enough. Here is the conclusion of Chapter 8 focusing on Rajesh writing to Leah:

That evening, Rajesh took out paper and pen by lamplight. As raindrops flowed down the window in rivulets, he poured his thoughts onto the page:

_My dearest Leah,_

_Home is quiet without your company to lift these walls with song and laughter. But speaking with Amma reminded me - all change begins another journey._

_Our time in Germany feels like a dream I cling to, full of discoveries and your smile that made each moment brighter. You opened my eyes to new landscapes and the beauty inside differences._

_Now as rains nourish spring's arrival, I take comfort that though far, our bond is timeless. Wherever this new season may lead, a part of my heart remains in your care._

_Until we meet again, may your days be bursting with joy, curiosity and the light that first drew me to you as sure as the north star. I promise, this is only the beginning of our story._

_Yours,_
_Rajesh_

Sealing the letter, he hoped one day their paths would weave together once more. For now, her memory was solace that theirs was a bond woven of life's richer threads, destined to remain intertwined however far the tides of time may take them. Here is the concluding passage for Chapter 8:

Rajesh walked to the post box under clearing skies, letter in hand. As he returned home, the first stars appeared along with flickers of lamps within mud-walled homes.

In his room, Rajesh took a framed photo from his bag - himself and Leah smiling under a blossom-filled bough in Germany's twilight. He placed it gently on his bedside table, brushing soft petals with a fond smile.

Though distant, she remained close to his heart in spirit and memory. As night fell and crickets sang, Rajesh drifted to dreams of adventures yet to come, knowing that for now, this photograph would watch over his slumber - a symbol of bond and promise that despite all, a piece of each other's hearts and stories were forever intertwined.

With that soothing thought, Chapter Eight drew to an end, as raindrops slowed to a calm and Rajesh's soul found rest, carried on wings of hope for what tomorrow may bring.

# Serendipitous Reunion

Rajesh immersed himself in tutoring as many students as he could in the village. While it was tiring work, he was determined to save every rupee to eventually further his studies abroad. He dreamed of the day he might reunite with Leah, perhaps pursuing graduate-level research alongside her inquisitive mind once more. Between sessions, Rajesh would often gaze at the letter she had sent, her words a balm to his longing.

"With diligence and hard work, all things are possible." Leah had written. Rajesh took those words to heart as he helped the local children navigate algebra equations and calculus derivatives. Though it had only been a few months since his return from Germany, he found solace in staying busy and maintaining their correspondence. In her latest letter, Leah mentioned potentially obtaining a scholarship for further chemistry studies at her university. Rajesh hoped that someday, their paths might cross again within the hallowed halls they both now considered a second home. One evening, as Rajesh was leaving the Kapoor household after tutoring their daughter Naina, Dr. Kapoor called out to him. "Rajesh, may I have a word?" he asked.

Rajesh went over to where Dr. Kapoor sat on the veranda, nervously anticipating what the well-respected doctor wanted. "Naina speaks very highly of your skills as a tutor. It is clear you have a gift for mathematics and an inquisitive mind," Dr. Kapoor began. "I understand you have been working diligently to save up funds to further your studies abroad one day. What if I told you I could sponsor your Ph.D. education at a top university in America?"

Rajesh's eyes widened in surprise. "Why me, sir?" he asked quietly.

Dr. Kapoor smiled. "I see your dedication and potential. You remind me of myself at your age. Let me support you as someone once did for me. With my backing, you can focus fully on your academics rather than worrying over costs. What do you say - will you accept this opportunity I am offering?"

Rajesh was at a loss for words. His dream of continuing his education alongside Leah might not be so far-fetched after all. Rajesh stood stunned, afraid to believe this was real. Dr. Kapoor's generosity was too much to comprehend.

"I-I do not know what to say, sir," Rajesh stammered. "This is an opportunity beyond my wildest dreams. To study at such a renowned university, with all expenses paid, is more than I could ever ask for."

Dr. Kapoor smiled kindly. "You need not ask - I am offering because I see your potential. So what do you think, will you accept?"

Rajesh swallowed back tears, overwhelmed with gratitude. "How can I ever thank you for this blessing, sir? I am but a simple village tutor. To have my education funded in this way is an honor I do not deserve."

"Nonsense," Dr. Kapoor replied. "You have worked hard and shown dedication to your studies. Now it is time the world witnessed your brilliance. The university I have in mind is where your German friend Leah is continuing her research, is it not?"

Rajesh gasped. It couldn't be - was the universe conspiring to reunite them once more? He took a shaky breath. "If it is truly your wish to support me, Dr. Kapoor, I accept with the deepest thanks. I will do my best to make you proud."

Dr. Kapoor smiled, placing a hand on Rajesh's shoulder. "I have no doubt you will excel, my boy. Now, let us discuss the details..." With trembling hands, Rajesh composed a letter to Leah sharing the incredible news. It took several drafts to find the words to describe the unexpected turn his life had taken. Once sealed, he rushed to post it, then spent the evening anxiously awaiting her response.

A few days later, Leah's neat script arrived. Rajesh tore it open eagerly, and her joyous exclamations leaped off the page. You accepted! I can hardly believe it—we'll be together once more! Of all the universities, wasn't it fate that it be mine? Leah couldn't contain her delight at the thought of having Rajesh by her side as they both furthered their studies.

Rajesh smiled at her infectious enthusiasm, feeling it lift his spirits. Reading her letter was like basking in her radiant presence again. He knew with Leah's encouragement, he would thrive in this new chapter. Despite the challenges ahead, he looked toward the future with anticipation, grateful that through kind individuals like Dr. Kapoor, even humble beginnings could lead to unimaginable gifts. Most of all, Rajesh savored Leah's excitement that their paths were destined to reunite once more. Rajesh's family gathered to see him off at the train station once more. His mother tightened her embrace, tears streaming. "My son is truly leaving the nest this time," she sighed.

Rajesh gave her hands a reassuring squeeze. "I will make you proud through my studies, Ma. And I promise to visit whenever I am able."

His brother-in-law gripped his shoulder proudly. "Go and spread your wings, Rajesh. We will be cheering you on."

Even his stern father placed a hand on his head. "Study diligently and represent our village well." It was as close to a blessing as Rajesh would receive.

As the train pulled into the station, he turned to his family gathered on the platform, smiling through misty eyes. "Thank you for believing in me. I will do my best."

With a final wave, Rajesh boarded, excited to begin this new adventure yet also feeling the bittersweet sting of parting from his roots once more. But the thought of seeing Leah's welcoming smile lifted his spirits. A new chapter was unfolding - one that would allow their stories to continue weaving together once more. Rajesh gazed out the plane window as America came into view, his heart filled with anticipation and wonder. When the airport came into sight, his pulse quickened at the realization of how close he was to seeing Leah again.

As he disembarked and entered the bustling terminal, Rajesh's palms grew damp with nervous energy. It had been so long since they stood side by side, would she still feel the same? Pushing down his doubts, Rajesh followed the signs for baggage claim.

Stepping outside, Rajesh froze at the sight of a familiar grin amidst the crowd. His breath caught in his throat as Leah rushed over, flinging her arms around him. He relaxed into her embrace, all worries melting away in her warmth.

They chatted eagerly during the drive to campus, catching up on the months apart. Leah's joy at having him near again set Rajesh's heart at ease. When the university gates came into view, he gazed at her with gratitude for making this foreign place feel like home once more. Their story was ready to unfold anew within hallowed halls that now held meaning for them both. Leah swung into Rajesh's arms the moment he exited the arrival terminal, abandoning her composure in a burst of joy. Rajesh laughed, twirling her in a circle as she peppered his face with kisses. At long last, they were together again.

As they drove to campus, their hands remained woven together on the seat. Lazy smiles and lingering gazes spoke the depths of their reunion. Leah regaled him with tales of breakthroughs in her research, while Rajesh told of monsoon clouds hanging heavy over his village fields.

Through it all, familiarity bloomed once more.

That evening, strolling through rose gardens alive with fireflies, Rajesh pulled Leah into an alcove hidden by twisting vines. Looking upon her dear face, he was overcome by the miracle of their reunion. Leah cupped his cheek and whispered how his presence lit her world anew each day. Their lips met gently, a promise of tomorrow destined to be shared.

Later as they parted at her door with a final embrace, joy spilled from Rajesh's heart. Here in America's green shores and within these hallowed halls, their future had blossomed once more after months of longing. Thanks to the blessings of kindred souls, love had found a way to seed hope where once was only solace in memory. Rajesh awoke the next day still unable to believe his fortune. As golden sunlight spilled across the bed where Leah still slept, he watched her eyelashes flutter and thought his heart may burst.

She greeted him with a sleepy smile, and he wondered how he'd survived so long without her morning glow. Over breakfast in the cafe they once treasured, the reality of her presence renewed his disbelief.

As they walked hand in hand to class, Leah paused to admire new blooms bursting from the earth. "Some destinies cannot be denied," she mused. Rajesh knew without doubt she spoke the truth. What were the chances fate would unite them here after mountains crossed and futures forged independently? Too great to be a coincidence.

Their eyes met and understanding passed without words. The seeds of their bond, watered by memory, had blossomed anew in this unexpected soil. As the campus green fluttered with butterfly wings, Rajesh believed in the serendipity that had brought them full circle once more.

# CHAPTER TEN

# Guided by Light

Rajesh immersed himself in his graduate studies, determined to make the most of this opportunity. However, as the semester progressed, he found himself drowning under the weight of advanced lectures and research expectations. Complex theorems that were once intuitive now caused headaches as he wrestled with proofs late into the night.

His collaboration with his research advisor was proving difficult as well. Where Rajesh possessed flashes of inventive insight, he struggled to articulate ideas in a coherent manner. Self-doubt crept in with each stuttered sentence and perplexed look from his advisor. Rajesh began to question if he truly belonged at this level of academia.

One evening, as Rajesh pored over dense texts on quantum algorithms, the equations blurred on the page. He rubbed his eyes wearily, remembering simpler lessons by lantern light in his village home. Doubt swirled in his mind - had he been fooling himself all along? Was he destined for simpler pursuits instead of lofty research?

His thoughts were interrupted by a soft knock. "Rajesh? It's getting late, please get some rest." Leah's kind eyes peered in, taking in his disheveled appearance. She grasped his struggles though he had shared few details. As always, her steadfast support anchored him during dark nights of the soul. Leah sat beside Rajesh and clasped his hands gently. "Your brilliant mind merely needs rest. Don't lose faith - you will overcome this hurdle as you've done so many times before."

Her words eased the tension in his shoulders, and Rajesh sighed. "But what if my limitations are finally clear? I feel incapable among these scholars."

"None of us journey alone. Let me help bear this weight, as you once did for me." Leah spoke softly of nights spent puzzling through problem sets together, learning from each other.

Her light touch lifted Rajesh's weary spirit. "You see potential where I see only inadequacy. I'm thankful for your belief in me."

Leah smiled. "Duty and gratitude keep us going when willpower fails. Now come, let us walk by the river - its currents soothe all troubles."

The swirling waters indeed calmed Rajesh's turbulence of mind. As fireflies flickered over still pools, Leah's fingers found his. Her affection rekindled hope that with patience and perseverance, he could navigate any darkness., Rajesh spent long hours at the library, digging through references on wave interference equations. But no matter which approach he tried, he hit a wall. Frustration clawed as one dead end led to another.

In a secluded corner, defeated, Rajesh dropped his head into his hands. No matter how hard he worked, was he doomed to fail where true geniuses thrived? He thought of his village, simple realities he understood. This world of theorems and abstractions seemed ever out of reach.

Leah found him there, withdrawn and brooding. Your gift lies not in what you've achieved, but courage to keep trying. True learning has no end; you must find joy in the struggle.

But I struggle alone while you effortlessly glide ahead. Her brow softened. My path was not effortless; I simply started sooner. Come, let us tackle this problem together as we've done before. Two minds often see more than one.

Their debate fueled a new perspective. By evening a breakthrough emerged, sparking Rajesh's creativity anew. Though the road remained long, Leah's partnership lightened the toil and rekindled tomorrow's hope. For now, in her steady light, he found solace and strength to face the trails that lay ahead., Here is the continuation focusing on the specified narrative beat:

As the days passed, Rajesh continued facing obstacles in his research. He grew frustrated with his perceived lack of progress, comparing himself to his peers. One evening, over a meal together, Leah noticed Rajesh's distress.

"What troubles you so?" she asked gently. Rajesh sighed. "No matter how hard I work, I feel far behind the others. I'm just not cut out for this level of study."

Leah regarded him thoughtfully. "Challenges don't determine destiny, they help sharpen great minds. Each problem you overcome makes the next hurdle easier to leap. Compare yourself not to others but to who you were yesterday."

Her words gave Rajesh pause. Was he allowing temporary setbacks to obscure hard-won gains?

Leah continued, "True learning happens not when knowledge comes easy, but when we push past discomfort. Have faith that struggle precedes triumph. You have come so far - don't doubt the strength and intellect that brought you here."

Her steadfast confidence lifted Rajesh's spirits. She was right - he had surmounted greater obstacles. With Leah's encouragement ringing in his ears, he felt a renewed resolve to keep climbing toward his goals. Here is the continuation focused on the specified narrative beat:

Leah's words sparked a renewed flame within Rajesh. She was right - he had overcome so much to get this far. Her unshakable belief in him reminded Rajesh of his strength and resolve.

The next day, Rajesh dove back into his research with a newfound motivation. Late into the night, he poured through texts and crafted equations with precise focus. Where there were gaps in his understanding, he asked probing questions of his colleagues until concepts crystallized.

On weekends, Rajesh sought Leah's counsel on particularly challenging problems. Their debates stretched into the early hours, fueled by a mutual passion for progress. Bit by bit, the pieces of his research puzzle started falling into place.

One evening, Rajesh excitedly shared a breakthrough with Leah over a meal. He beamed with pride as she congratulated his success. Her faith in him was his wind beneath weary wings - with her steadfast support, any mountain seemed scalable.

From that day, Rajesh's confidence and intellect blossomed thanks to Leah's guidance. He redoubled efforts each day, determined to prove the aptitude she saw within him. With Leah by his side, Rajesh felt empowered to conquer any academic challenge and fulfill his potential., Here is the continuation focused on the specified narrative beat:

Weeks of diligent study bore fruit as Rajesh tackled the most challenging proof in his research. Late one night, fueled by coffee, he pushed through mental block after block until the equations flowed seamlessly.

As the final steps intuitively fell into place, Rajesh saw with startling clarity the elegance of the solution. He stared in awe, hardly daring to believe the breakthrough in his grasp. Joy and astonishment swept through him- all those hours of struggle had led to this moment of triumph.

The next morning, Rajesh rushed to share the proof with his research group, breathless with excitement. His advisor studied the elegantly constructed steps with scrutiny before breaking into a proud smile. This is superb work, Rajesh - a true academic achievement. His praise echoed in the halls as word spread of Rajesh's breakthrough.

That evening, Rajesh and Leah celebrated the breakthrough over a private dinner. He glowed with well-earned pride recounting each step revealed. You've more than proven your mettle, she said gently. I always knew greatness resided within you, waiting to be unveiled. Rajesh marveled at her faith, the ignition of his blossoming potential. At long last, he felt like he truly belonged among intellectual greats, thanks to Leah's guidance and support. Here is the continuation focused on the specified narrative beat:

That evening, Rajesh and Leah went out to celebrate his breakthrough. Over a candlelit dinner at their favorite restaurant by the river, they recounted the journey that led to this triumphant moment.

Rajesh beamed as he told Leah how her guidance and reassurance lifted him during his darkest doubts. Without your belief in me, I would have lost my way, he said with emotion. Leah took his hands in hers, her eyes glowing with admiration. I only shone a little light - the achievement was all yours through hard work and perseverance.

As they walked along the riverbank afterward, fingers entwined, Rajesh felt at peace. Leah's presence filled him with joy and lightened any burden. He turned to her tenderly, grateful beyond words. You are my pillar of strength and inspiration. I couldn't have come this far without your steadfast support.

Leah smiled, a warmth in her eyes that came only for him. Your gift was there waiting within to be honed through challenge and focus. I'm proud to witness your brilliance unveiled. Their kiss under the stars was Sweet with victory and promise of greater things to come through their enduring bond., Here is the conclusion to Chapter 10 focused on the specified narrative beat:

As Rajesh walked Leah home that night, he could hardly contain his joy and gratitude. Her unwavering faith in him gave Rajesh strength when his own faltered. Time and again she had proven the most staunch believer in his abilities.

Leah turned to Rajesh with a gentle smile by her door. I'm so proud to see your light shine for all to witness. Your perseverance is an inspiration.

Rajesh took her hands and brought them to his lips. Without your support from the moment we met, I would never have made it this far. You saw my potential even when I doubted, and your encouragement pushed me to fulfill my promise. You are the shining north star that guides me.

Leah embraced him close, her eyes gleaming. And I will continue cheering your journey, wherever it may lead. Now rest - there is yet more brilliance to unleash upon the world.

As Rajesh drifted to sleep that night, quiet gratitude surged in his heart for the woman who planted the seeds of his success through compassion and faith in his capabilities. Leah's enduring support lit his path and empowered him to ever-greater achievements.

# Navigating Doubt, Love, and Destiny

Weeks passed productively until a complex theorem stymied Rajesh's efforts. Late nights in the library yielded no breakthrough. His mind spun in exhausted circles as doubt's shadow lengthened.

One evening, poring over reference texts yet finding no answers, Rajesh slammed his fist in frustration. All around him, other scholars worked undaunted while the problem that was simple to them taunted him. He leaned back, rubbing his eyes hard.

What if this proves my limit? What if I'm not truly meant for this level of study after all?

Footsteps approached. "Rajesh?" Leah's soft voice roused him from the darkness's edge.

He sighed. "This theorem defeats me at every turn. While others progress unimpeded, I'm left grasping at phantoms."

Leah squeezed his hand. "Genius takes many forms. Where

logic fails, intuition may find a way. Come, a walk will clear your head for a fresh start tomorrow."

Her trust in him gave solace, yet the theorem's insolubility gnawed as a dead end appeared, challenging his place among scholars. But with Leah by his side, he took heart to continue., Here is a continuation following the specified beat:

The next day, Rajesh dove back into textbooks with renewed focus. Hours blurred until sunset's glow through high windows reminded him of his plans with Leah.

He dashed to their usual cafe, breathless with apology. "I lost track of time in my studies. Please, forgive -"

Leah merely smiled. "I'm glad to see that thoughtful look has returned to your eyes. All is well so long as we're together now."

Her gentle acceptance eased his worry. They supped on chicken curry and naan, conversing through the meal. Rajesh related his further research ideas to glean new angles on the theorem. Leah listened with her usual keen insight, then spoke of her day's adventures to lighten his serious mood.

As they walked out into the rose-gold twilight, Leah tucked her hand in the crook of his arm. "However consumed you become in theorems, know that you need only be present with me to find peace. Now, come - I spied a blossoming magnolia we must admire beneath the stars."

Her unwavering care and faith in him nourished Rajesh's spirit each day, restoring strength for the continued pursuit of understanding through their affection., Here is a continuation following the specified beat:

That weekend, Rajesh took Leah to her favorite bistro by the river. As they dined on creamy pasta and crisp greens under twinkling lights, conversation flowed easily from campus news to childhood recollections.

Rajesh watched Leah's gestures animatedly, relishing her insights and laughter. A warmth arose unbidden in his chest at the thought of many more such evenings together. Beyond scholastic partnership, he realized Leah had become as vital to his heart as air.

Her empathy and quick mind matched his own, supporting his dreams while challenging preconceptions with refreshing perspectives. At her side, all avenues of learning seemed to open. More than that - with Leah, he felt complete.

As their eyes met across flickering candles, Rajesh took Leah's hands in his. "My dearest, these years with you have been a blessing beyond words. I can envision no future without your presence lighting my way. Will you do me the honor of becoming my wife, to walk alongside me not just in life but in its pursuit of deeper truths?"

Leah's smile shone like radiant starlight, stealing his breath away. "Oh, Rajesh, there is no one else I would rather have by my side on such a journey. Yes, with all my heart - yes!"

Their kiss was filled with joy and promise as surrounding trees whispered a benediction on their new beginning. All the world seemed aglow with possibility in Leah's exultant eyes. Here is a continuation following the specified beat:

Leah's delighted yes echoed in Rajesh's heart as they walked hand in hand down lamp-lit sidewalks. Above, a tapestry of stars glittered through sparse clouds, as if sharing in their joy.

At her door, Rajesh held Leah close, loath to part yet content in her nearness. All are aligned - my work finds purpose and fulfillment, my life purpose in you. For the first time, a future appears certain and bright.

Leah caressed his cheek, gazing at him with stars reflected in her eyes. You have worked so hard to get here, my love, and deserve every reward. I look forward to standing by your side as an equal partner in all things, sharing both successes and struggles. Our adventure has only just begun!

Reluctantly drawing away, Rajesh lifted her hand to kiss it, lingering. Until tomorrow, my light. Sleep well.

He walked home under a starry sky awash in peace, for his heart and mind had found anchorage and purpose intertwined. At long last, professional aspiration and personal joy converged, bringing a serenity that allowed even challenges to pall before hope for all the learning, loving years unfolding ahead., Here is a continuation following the specified beat:

While Rajesh and Leah's bond grew deeper, not all met

their engagement with joy. Some colleagues questioned if marriage may distract from their scholarly pursuits, sowing unwanted seeds of doubt.

One evening, as pressures mounted, Rajesh and Leah walked along the river in pensive silence. At last, Rajesh sighed. "Perhaps they speak the truth - our duties to research should come before all else."

Leah stopped and turned to face him, emerald eyes stern yet kind. "Rajesh, look at me. I did not agree to stand beside you as anything less than an equal partner, in success and strife alike. Our commitment strengthens, not weakens our purpose. As long as we have each other's loyalty, no outer disapproval can sway our course. Do you still want me by your side through all the challenges to come?"

At her words, Rajesh's worries vanished like mist. Taking her hands, he smiled with newfound resolve. "You're right, my love - together, no obstacle can deter us from our shared aims. Your support sustains me as does mine you. From this day forth our bond comes before all else. The world may question, but our faith alone needs an answer."

Hand in hand they walked on, secure in the sanctuary of their devotion despite whispers meant to shake it. With Leah as his strength, motivation, and solace combined, Rajesh embarked on his journey anew, fortified. Here is a conclusion to Chapter 11 following the specified beat:

That night, as Rajesh parted from Leah at her door, he gazed at her silhouette in the lamplight, awash in tenderness. How blessed he felt that fate drew them back together across vast distances, her light now his anchor in all of life's varied seas.

Taking her hands, Rajesh pressed them to his lips with grateful reverence. My stars, how lucky I am to call you mine. In a world filled with strangers, you have walked by my side as my kindest comfort and dearest friend. I will spend my days proving worthy of the love you bear me.

Leah's smile held galaxies as she wound her arms around his neck. My dear Rajesh, it was you alone who gave color and meaning to my days from the first. Every step brings us closer to the dreams we share. Now go in peace, and know that you are the light that guides my every footfall in turn.

Their kiss spoke all the devotion words could not hold. As Rajesh walked home under a tapestry of shining stars, the peace of Leah's faithful presence encircled him with infinite gratitude for the partner fate had granted him to walk beside through every joy, trial, and revelation on the horizon.

# CHAPTER TWELVE

# Shattered Dreams

Leah's delighted yes echoed in Rajesh's heart as they walked hand in hand down lamp-lit sidewalks. Above, a tapestry of stars glittered through sparse clouds, as if sharing in their joy.

At her door, Rajesh held Leah close, loath to part yet content in her nearness. All is aligned - my work finds purpose and fulfillment, my life purpose in you. For the first time, a future appears certain and bright.

Leah caressed his cheek, gazing at him with stars reflected in her eyes. You have worked so hard to get here, my love, and deserve every reward. I look forward to standing by your side as an equal partner in all things, sharing both successes and struggles. Our adventure has only just begun!

Reluctantly drawing away, Rajesh lifted her hand to kiss it, lingering. Until tomorrow, my light. Sleep well.

He walked home under a starry sky awash in peace, for his heart and mind had found anchorage and purpose intertwined. At long last, professional aspiration and personal joy converged, bringing a serenity that allowed even challenges to pall before hope for all the learning, loving years unfolding ahead., Here is a continuation following the specified beat:

While Rajesh and Leah's bond grew deeper, not all met their engagement with joy. Some colleagues questioned if marriage may distract from their scholarly pursuits, sowing unwanted seeds of doubt.

One evening, as pressures mounted, Rajesh and Leah walked along the river in pensive silence. At last, Rajesh sighed. "Perhaps they speak the truth - our duties to research should come before all else."

Leah stopped and turned to face him, emerald eyes stern yet kind. "Rajesh, look at me. I did not agree to stand beside you as anything less than an equal partner, in success and strife alike. Our commitment strengthens, not weakens our purpose. As long as we have each other's loyalty, no outer disapproval can sway our course. Do you still want me by your side through all the challenges to come?"

At her words, Rajesh's worries vanished like mist. Taking her hands, he smiled with newfound resolve. "You're right, my love - together, no obstacle can deter us from our shared aims. Your support sustains me as does mine you. From this day forth our bond comes before all else. The world may question, but our faith alone needs an answer."

Hand in hand they walked on, secure in the sanctuary of their devotion despite whispers meant to shake it. With Leah as his strength, motivation, and solace combined, Rajesh embarked on his journey anew, fortified. Here is a conclusion to Chapter 11 following the specified beat:

That night, as Rajesh parted from Leah at her door, he gazed at her silhouette in the lamplight, awash in tenderness. How blessed he felt that fate drew them back together across vast distances, her light now his anchor in all of life's varied seas.

Taking her hands, Rajesh pressed them to his lips with grateful reverence. My stars, how lucky I am to call you mine. In a world filled with strangers, you have walked by my side as my kindest comfort and dearest friend. I will spend my days proving worthy of the love you bear me.

Leah's smile held galaxies as she wound her arms around his neck. My dear Rajesh, it was you alone who gave color and meaning to my days from the first. Every step brings us closer to the dreams we share. Now go in peace, and know that you are the light that guides my every footfall in turn.

Their kiss spoke all the devotion words could not hold. As Rajesh walked home under a tapestry of shining stars, the peace of Leah's faithful presence encircled him with infinite gratitude for the partner fate had granted him to walk beside through every joy, trial, and revelation on the horizon. His journey had only begun. I apologize, but there does not appear to be any additional narrative beats specified for Chapter 11 in the reference material provided. The 8 beats outlined previously conclude the chapter's events as described in the story outline. Unless another beat is specified, I do not have any additional details to continue the narrative for this chapter. Please provide another narrative beat or indication to proceed to wrap up

Chapter 11 and transition to the next chapter. Rajesh woke to the light peeking through the curtains and the smell of coffee brewing. He lay awake for a moment, treasuring these quiet mornings with Leah before the bustle of the day began.

Stretching with a contented sigh, he followed the aroma into the kitchen. Leah smiled over her mug. "Good morning, darling. The coffee's fresh."

They enjoyed a leisurely breakfast, stealing smiles and light touches between bites. Too soon, it was time for their separate classes. At the door, Rajesh pulled Leah close. "Dinner tonight? I'll pick up ingredients for carbonara."

"Perfect. Don't work too hard." She kissed him goodbye.

The day passed swiftly in busy lecture halls. At last, Rajesh arrived home laden with grocery bags. Leah greeted him with a hug, still dressed in her lab coat.

Over a meal and laughter, they recounted assignments and research problems solved. Leah was his fiercest champion, and her caring ear eased Rajesh's stresses. In return, he cheered her successes with warmth and pride.

Later, curled together on the couch, Rajesh marveled at the fortune that brought this wonderful woman into his life. Leah kissed him softly and rested her head on his chest, over his steady heartbeat. There, in each other's arms, the trials of the day faded into quiet joy. Their relationship bloomed through understanding, and so Leah saw Rajesh's tiredness after long nights working. Still, she wanted to celebrate their love, so she planned a special anniversary dinner.

Between classes, she shopped for fresh salmon and wild rice. Sunflowers, their early picnic flowers, brightened the table. Leah arrived home exhausted but content. As Rajesh hugged her hello, she said, "Dinner's almost ready, but first - close your eyes."

At the table, scented with rosemary, she uncovered their meal with a pleased smile. "Happy anniversary, my heart. This is to remind you how much you mean to me, especially when life feels heavy."

Rajesh embraced hertenderly. "Your thoughtfulness is all I need. Being with you lifts my spirit above any troubles." They dined with hands clasped, exchanging loving smiles and memories of when their hearts first met under blossoming trees.

Through each challenge, they supported each other. Their bond was anchored in compassion, and in Leah's care, Rajesh found strength. Rajesh worked later than intended, but nothing could stop him from celebrating with Leah. He rushed to finish, barely pausing for breath as equations flew across the board.

Gathering his things, Rajesh burst into the cool evening and began the swift journey home. Darkness fell as he walked, only one thought playing in his mind - he couldn't disappoint her.

The apartment came into view all too soon, and Rajesh

feared he was late. But looking up, he saw Leah in their window, the faithful candle still burning as she watched and waited.

Her face lit up seeing him. You made it! I'm so glad. They embraced, his hurried steps forgotten in her caring arms. Over a shared dessert, Rajesh apologized for losing track of time. But Leah silenced him with a kiss. Your passion for learning is one of the reasons I love you. Now, let's focus on us.

Their fingers laced, hearts intertwined, as they watched the city lights under starry skies. All was well, for in each other's presence, home is wherever they are together. Rajesh was rushed to the hospital, heart in his throat. A nurse met him, face dark with sorrow. He knew then but needed to hear the words.

The doctor emerged, eyes heavy. I'm afraid Ms. Leah didn't make it. Her injuries...there was nothing we could do. She didn't suffer. Rajesh barely heard over the thundering inside his skull.

It couldn't be real - just yesterday they watched the sunset, skin touching and futures glowing. But the sterile halls echoed truth in every footstep. He entered her vacant room, a scene of so many quiet talks, and it struck him: she was gone.

Crumpling to the floor, raw anguish tore from his lips in an agonized howl that echoed his very soul being rent. Strong arms lifted him, trying to offer comfort, but no solace could mend the crushing void left by Leah's light extinguished much too soon.

All meaning bled away. Rajesh's tears did not relent, grieving freely for his greatest love now lost to this world. His heart was shattered, and in its broken pieces, it vowed: never again would it open whole to another so completely. The pain was too vast, cut too deep., Rajesh could not stand - his legs buckled beneath the abyss of grief. He hit the floor hard but felt no pain. Physical hurt was nothing to the agony rending his heart and soul.

Great, heaving sobs burst from his hollow chest as he clutched desperately at the tiles. Why her? It wasn't fair - they had so much more to share, adventures ahead dancing in their eyes only yesterday.

Now those eyes would never light with mirth again. The lips he kissed in the promise of forever were forever stilled. Her hands, which caressed his cheek with such care, would no longer soothe away his worries.

Through his tears, Rajesh howled her name like a wounded animal. Leah! Please, my heart, come back to me! But there was only suffocating silence in reply.

All the bright futures they dreamed of in quiet moments crumbled to dust before his eyes. Her memory was now the most vivid - all else had gone grey and dismal. His sole reason for being was torn cruelly away without mercy or reason.

Rajesh wept until he had no tears left to give. Still, the agony clawed at his insides. In that cold, sterile place, he mourned all that might have been forever lost to the darkness now descending upon his destroyed world. Rajesh pulled himself to Leah's side on leaden limbs. Gently, shakily, he took her limp hand in his, finding it cold as ice. A hollow shell where his vibrant girl once resided.

"Please, my love," he croaked, brushing back her hair. Everything about her was still, devoid of the lively spirit within. "Open your eyes. I'm here - come back to me now."

But her eyes did not flutter, gazing blankly at nothing. A sob wracked Rajesh's frame, agony pouring out with every ragged breath. "Don't leave me alone, Leah! I can't do this without you...I need you."

He collapsed over her still form, shoulders shaking with grief. Her perfume still clung to her skin but couldn't mask the dread scent of finality. Clutching her close, Rajesh allowed his tears to fall freely once more.

"You promised me forever." His voice was but a shattered whisper. "Please, my heart, I'm not ready to say goodbye...I love you."

Only silence answered his plea. Leah's soul had fled, leaving Rajesh cradling her mortal remains as her warmth faded, and his dreams turned to ash. Rajesh wandered the dim streets in a daze, one foot mechanically in front of the other. Leah's empty bed awaited but he couldn't face it yet.

Her memory was everywhere - each place they passed held an echo. Here they strolled hand in hand, there she threw her head back in laughter. If he closed his eyes, her smile was as vivid as ever.

But the bitter truth invaded again and again. Leah was gone. She would never greet him at the doorway after a long day, never embrace him, and breathe life back into his soul. The future they planned in hushed tones now belonged only to his broken dreams.

Rajesh replayed their last kiss over and over, clinging to her fading warmth and touch. But try as he might, he couldn't outpace the frigid fingers of denial curling around his throat. Leah was gone. Gone. His love, his light, was torn away in an instant without mercy or farewell.

Despair threatened to drown him where he stood. Staggering at last to their apartment, Rajesh collapsed into her pillow and wept anew as familiar scents wrapped tight around his ravaged heart. But no matter how many tears fell, they couldn't change cruel Fate's design. Leah was gone, and Rajesh was utterly alone. Rajesh curled into himself, clutching Leah's pillow to his ravaged chest. Her absence was a phantom pain that stole his every breath. Outside, the city moved on but within these walls, grief held dominion over his crushed spirit.

A tormented sound ripped from his throat as heartbreak overwhelmed him in waves. Tears flowed freely once more, his body wracked with the force of his raw anguish. Rajesh screamed his agony into the silent room, the echoes mocking in their futility.

Nobody could hear - he was utterly alone. Leah had been his everything, the light that guided his steps and lifted his soul. Now shadows descended where she once shone so brightly, cold and unforgiving.

Rajesh howled her name until his voice grew hoarse, begging her ghost for solace that would never come. His tears soaked the pillow, mourning all the moments stolen away by cruel fate. How could he go on in this grim half-life without her? The darkness was suffocating.

Exhausted but finding no release, Rajesh wept himself into a fitful slumber. Even in dreams, she haunted him, always just beyond reach. He was lost without her, adrift on an endless sea of misery as loneliness devoured him from within.

# CHAPTER THIRTEEN

# Nadir

The weeks passed in a haze for Rajesh. He drifted through each day like a ghost, barely noticing his surroundings. His small apartment remained dim, the curtains drawn as if to block out the world. Rajesh moved mechanically from room to room, not seeing or thinking. All sense of purpose and direction had vanished along with Leah's radiant smile.

His classes and research went untouched. Letters and phone calls from concerned friends and family went unanswered. Rajesh barely ate or slept, losing track of time as he replayed memories of Leah on an endless loop in his mind. Her vibrant laughter echoed in the silence, only making her absence feel more profound.

Everywhere Rajesh looked there were reminders of what he had lost. The books on his shelf were the ones they had enjoyed discussing. Photos of their travels together stared mournfully from frames. The nights they had spent curled together on the couch now felt unbearably lonely.

Rajesh wandered through a gray world of his own making, unable and unwilling to face a future without Leah by his side. She had brought such light and color into his life, and now he existed in her shadow, paralyzed by the weight of his grief. He knew others worried for him, but their well-meaning words could not penetrate the numbness or ease his anguish. Nothing mattered anymore except preserving Leah's memory from the ravages of time. Dev knocked gently on Rajesh's door, though he knew his friend would not answer. Still, he persisted, hoping that one day soon Rajesh might be ready to let someone in. "I've brought food," he called softly. "Please eat something, my brother. You cannot go on like this."

There was only silence from within. Dev leaned his head against the door with a heavy sigh. How could he ease Rajesh's suffering when he was barricaded both physically and emotionally? It pained Dev to see his once-vibrant friend reduced to a shadow, but Rajesh pushed away all help as though drowning in his private ocean of grief.

Not for the first time, Dev cursed the fickle hand of fate that had stolen Leah away so cruelly. She alone had possessed the ability to draw Rajesh into the light once more. Without her radiance, Rajesh remained lost in the darkness of despair, clinging stubbornly to his anguish as though it were the last connection to his beloved.

For now, all Dev could do was leave provisions and assurances of his support, hoping Rajesh would eventually accept the outstretched hands ready to lift him from the mire of his mourning. But until then, the inscrutable depths of grief held Rajesh fast, leaving him locked away in a prison one where no comfort could penetrate the walls of his solitary agony. All they could do was wait and pray that Rajesh finds his way back from the shadows in his own time. Rajesh stared dully at the books and papers strewn across his desk, once a source of intrigue and challenge but now as bleak and lifeless as the dreary world beyond his walls. The theorems and equations that had fueled his passion for knowledge now seemed pointless riddles conceived merely to torment him further. Without Leah by his side to share discoveries and debate ideas, what was the point of any of it?

His research sat abandoned and unfinished, a crumbling monument to all they had hoped to achieve together. Each page was stained with tears shed as realizations of her absence struck fresh blows. There was no solace to be found anymore in the concepts that had defined his life and drawn them close. Only emptiness remained where inspiration and purpose had been.

With great finality, Rajesh gathered his notes and manuscripts, piling them carelessly into a box without a backward glance. His research advisor's repeated warnings that he was throwing away his gifts echoed distantly, but Rajesh was past caring about anything but preserving Leah's memory. He no longer wished to delve into theorems or expand learning - he simply wished to fade from the world as fully as his heart had when she left it forever. Closing the lid of the box, Rajesh shut out his former life along with it, leaving the pieces of his shattered purpose locked firmly in the past where Leah still lived on in his mind., Rajesh drifted through another gray day in a haze of grief and detachment. Stubble shaded his hollow cheeks and unwashed hair fell lank around his sunken eyes. His clothes hung loose like a forgotten shroud, evidence of numerous meals skipped in favor of crumpled takeout containers strewn about like dead leaves.

The stagnant apartment absorbed his neglect and misery, an outward reflection of Rajesh's internal decay. Dishes piled high in the sink while dust gathered undisturbed. Only patches of the wooden floor remained visible under the clutter of discarded clothes, half-empty mugs, and stray notebooks bearing the remnants of thoughts that now seemed as meaningless as Rajesh's existence.

He moved through the squalor like a wounded animal seeking its den, consciousness blurred by sorrow and physical needs ignored. What did basic hygiene or self-care matter when the light that had illuminated his world was forever extinguished? All that remained was an empty shell inhabited by a grieving ghost, wasting away amid the ruins of a life interrupted by fate's cold hand. Rajesh existed in a permanent twilight, lost in his memories and indifferent to a world that had never seemed less real or felt more unbearably lonely. His apartment served only as a tomb for the man he had been before loss remade him into this despondent phantom drifting directionless through each bleak day. The incessant ringing cut through Rajesh's fog like a dull knife. With a grunt, he fumbled for his phone, squinting at the flashing name. Dev. Again. Rajesh sighed, debating ignoring it once more, but Dev's persistence wore him down. "What?" he rasped.

"My brother, please." Dev's weariness seeped through the line. "Come home. This place only prolongs your pain. Among familiar faces, your heart may find solace."

Home. An alien concept now. There was no home without

Leah. But Dev's concern chipped at Rajesh's armor. He knew his friend mourned seeing him like this. "I cannot," Rajesh murmured, staring blankly at the peeling wallpaper.

Dev exhaled slowly. "You cannot remain lost forever. Leah would not wish to see you waste away. Her love still lights your path, even if you cannot yet see it. Come, walk with me again under the warm sun. Let family soothe your wounds."

Rajesh said nothing for a long while, but the tightness in his chest eased, and he sighed. Everything was hazy, but Dev's care cut through the fog. Perhaps among family, the throbbing ache in his soul could start to heal. "Very well, brother. I will return." Rajesh dragged himself to his computer with leaden limbs. His searches yielded countless flights, but the thought of boarding alone filled him with dread. Still, Dev's plea echoed in his mind. With a resigned sigh, Rajesh booked the first available ticket, wanting this ordeal over.

Packing proved more difficult than imagined. Every belonging seemed tied to a memory with Leah. Her favorite sweater still carried faint hints of jasmine. Photos captured private smiles are now bittersweet. Rajesh packed methodically, each item a tiny burial of a life cut short.

As the apartment emptied, echoes of carefree voices grew louder in the barren rooms. This place had been their retreat, filled with hopes for a shared future now out of reach. Leaving it marked another nail in the coffin of dreams entombed with Leah's memory.

The departure date loomed like a prison sentence, but Rajesh knew stasis would not mend his tattered soul. Perhaps familiar sights might provide solace where foreign walls had compounded his loneliness. Yet facing life alone terrified him more than any nightmare conjured by insomnia's ruthless grasp. Each step would be waded through a river of grief toward an unknown bare of Leah's light. All Rajesh could do was endure, one foot shakily placed before the other. Rajesh rode to the airport in a haze, mechanically submitting his luggage for departure. As he wandered the terminal, each laugh or embrace of reunited travelers pierced his anesthetized heart. Boarding commenced in a blur of color and motion, but Rajesh felt frozen still, left behind in an empty life strapped down for takeoff.

He sank numbly into his seat, gazing unseeingly at a sky that had held so many hopes. Their plans for adventures, discoveries, and milestones are scattered among the clouds like dandelion clocks, drifting farther each moment. Now Rajesh joined their restless wandering, unmoored from dreams last whispered against Leah's temple under a dreaming sky.

As the engines roared, Rajesh felt the vibrations deep in his core, the only reminder he still lived while Leah's light flickered out. His hand clenched painfully on the armrest as the land fell away, carrying his heart still somewhere below. This flight separated him from only rotting memories where joy once grew wild and unrestrained. All delight had flown from Rajesh's grasp, leaving behind a hollow shell strapped into place for a journey he wished never to take alone. Rajesh shut his eyes against gathering sting, plunging into darkness with nothing to see or want of tomorrow's rising sun. Rajesh moved through crowded airport corridors in a daze, barely noticing the familiar colors and sounds of home. His name echoed faintly somewhere ahead, but all sensation felt muffled behind a thick pane of glass.

There they waited - mother, brothers, everyone - faces alight with mingled worry and welcome. But when they embraced Rajesh, he remained stiff and unresponsive as a mannequin in their clinging arms. Their voices blended to an indistinct hum while concerned eyes scanned his haggard form for any signs of life remaining beneath the shell.

Rajesh let himself be guided through the terminal, viewing each reunion through a deepening fog. Joyful reunions and tearful greetings seemed to unfold underwater, beautiful and terrible all at once in their inaccessibility behind the barrier enclosing his depleted spirit.

The ride passed in wordless agony, Rajesh slumped against the humming window staring blankly ahead while his mother cast him sidelong glances overflowing with grief for the son who had returned but not truly come home. When they arrived, Rajesh wandered the familiar streets as a phantom, cut off even from himself with no comfort in familiarity now that the lifeblood had been leached from his ghostly veins by sorrow's ruthless attack. Home was no balm to his ravaged soul; no place on earth could fill the void or mend the terrible emptiness within. Rajesh drifted onward, untethered, through a world that had lost all warmth, purpose, and meaning in Leah's eternal absence.

# CHAPTER FOURTEEN

# Rays of Hope

Rajesh drifted through his days in a haze of grief. Since returning to his village, he taught his classes in a detached manner, going through the motions without feeling. The bright light that had illuminated his world was now gone, leaving darkness in its wake. He lived like a ghost in his dimly lit apartment, rarely venturing outside except for his teaching duties at the school.

In the evenings, he poured over manuscripts and mathematical texts by lamplight, submerging himself in complex equations and proofs in an attempt to fill the void in his heart. But no amount of study could take away the ache of Leah's absence or soothe his anguished soul. He lived numbly from day to day, withdrawing further into himself as memories of her invaded his mind. Without Leah's radiant smile and encouraging presence, Rajesh's world seemed drained of meaning and color. Her death had left him shattered, pieces of his heart strewn across continents with no hope of being made whole again. On some nights, in a desperate bid to escape his pain, Rajesh would drink himself into an empty, dreamless sleep. But reality always returned to torment him with his loss. Wandering alone through the ruins of his former self,

Rajesh surrendered to the darkness that now consumed his days. Aditi was one of Rajesh's brightest students. Where the others raced to complete their assignments and leave, she stayed behind asking thoughtful questions that demonstrated her keen aptitude. One evening, as Rajesh was gathering his things after class, she lingered with a curious expression.

"Sir, may I ask about the proof we discussed today? There was one step I did not fully understand."

Rajesh paused tiredly, having lost interest in his work long ago. But something in Aditi's attentive gaze drew him in. He explained the concept again, surprised by her intuitive grasp of advanced topics. Aditi countered with insightful observations, and their discussion deepened. For the first time in months, Rajesh felt a spark of interest taking hold.

They fell into such engaging debates regularly. While others had long given up on eliciting a response, Aditi persisted with her respectful inquiries. Carrying stacks of books, she walked with Rajesh often, chatting about theorem and postulate alike. Her gentle encouragement reminded Rajesh of seeking truth for its own sake, not prestige - a lesson he thought lost until her thoughtful presence reawoke it., Aditi noticed subtle changes in her reserved teacher. Where once he spoke passionately of mathematical discoveries, now he floated through lectures like a ghost. Seeing Rajesh packed to leave one evening, she worked up the courage to ask softly -

Sir, are you well? I sense there is sadness beneath your words.

Rajesh paused, surprised by her perceptiveness. No one had dared broach his pain in months.

You are observant, Aditi. I have endured a great loss that I cannot shake off.

Without judgement, she replied - I understand grief's weight all too well, sir. My mother also left this world too soon. If you'd like a ear, I'm here to listen.

Her sincere empathy touched Rajesh. Perhaps this student saw deeper than most, able to piece together his fractured exterior. He owed her honesty.

I lost someone who gave my life bright purpose. Now all seems dark, he admitted wearily.

With gentle eyes and kind heart, Aditi offered the solace of her presence. Her wisdom belied her youth, reminding Rajesh that from darkness, light may yet emerge., Rajesh was unused to sharing his private pains, keeping them locked tightly within. Yet Aditi's gentle nature disarmed his reservations, and he began cautiously opening up during their walks after class.

At first, he spoke only of mathematical pursuits, theories that once fueled his passion. Aditi listened attentively, asking thoughtful questions to draw him out. Steadily, he fondly recalled memories of village life and university years, the loved ones who guided his journey.

Bit by bit, he revealed more of his time in Germany - the

vibrant discussions, picnics by flowing streams, and most of all, Leah's radiant spirit that revived his soul. Speaking of her for the first time in months stirred bittersweet recollections, yet brought surprising solace. Aditi seemed to understand without needing explanations, her quiet empathy soothing his troubled heart.

One evening, over fragrant chai, Rajesh found himself reciting Leah's favorite poems and describing the park where they strolled. His eyes misted at the vivid sights, sounds and scents suddenly surrounding him through the mists of memory. But rather than look away, Aditi listened closely, gently encouraging him to linger in moments that seemed to heal rather than hurt. Her compassion lifted his spirit to heights he had not known since his beloved's loss. Rajesh began to glimpse light where once dwelled only shadows. One evening, as they sat speaking by a quiet pond, Aditi revealed her own secret grief.

"I too know the ache of loss," she began quietly. "My dearest friend Shreya passed away last year in an accident. We had grown up side by side and she was like family to me."

Rajesh listened intently, realizing for the first time the depth of understanding beneath Aditi's gentle eyes.

"The days seemed dark without her bright spirit. I withdrew from the world as you did. But Shreya would not have wanted me to lose hope." Aditi continued.

"Through our talks, she guided me to see life's beauty still remained, even in times of deepest sorrow. Now I try to pay her kindness forward, to offer an ear without judgment."

Rajesh grasped Aditi's hand gently. "You have shown me such empathy. I am grateful beyond words for your compassion."

Aditi's smile held warmth but no pretense. Through sharing her story, she had bridged the distance between them, allowing Rajesh's wounded heart to feel understood in its grief., Rajesh spoke often of Leah during his walks with Aditi, sharing fond memories and cherished moments from their time together. At first, the memories had threatened to overwhelm him with sorrow. But speaking of her to gentle Aditi's listening ear released their healing power.

He found he could smile through the tears as he recalled Leah's bright laugh echoing through the university corridors. Or the thoughtful debates they would engage in over steaming cups of coffee. As Aditi listened with quiet empathy, Rajesh realized the bittersweet beauty in remembering.

His beloved's vibrant spirit lived on through the stories he told. And in sharing them, the burden of grief felt lighter for the first time since her passing. He was grateful to Aditi for creating a safe space where sorrow need not exist alone, constricted, and crushing, but could breathe and evolve freely into remembrance.

"You help me see I do not have to bear this pain by myself," he said to Aditi one evening, as they watched the sunset spread orange and pink across the horizon. Her gentle smile held only compassion. Through opening his heart, Rajesh was learning darkness did not have to reign forever, and from kindness, light may yet emerge. Aditi's steadfast compassion gradually began penetrating the shadowy grief that had enshrouded Rajesh's heart. As he freely shared memories and found solace in her listening silence, a change came over him.

The old spark of curiosity that had fueled his lifelong pursuit of knowledge was slowly rekindling. On their walks, when Aditi posed thoughtful questions about his lectures, Rajesh found himself again delving deeply into mathematical concepts and theorems as in his youthful university days.

Engaging with her insightful mind revived Rajesh's passion for discovery. He began preparing thoroughly for his lessons instead of meandering through them. Aditi noticed his lessons coming alive with the enthusiasm she recalled from their early interactions.

One evening, she remarked on the light returning to his eyes. Rajesh realized with quiet wonder that speaking of loved ones lost need not keep the past alive in pain alone, but could nurture joy in lives fully lived too. Through her kindness, a glimmer of hope had penetrated the shadows of his grieving heart, stirring motivation once more. Her gentle guidance was helping him heal. Aditi's inquisitive nature spurred Rajesh to impart mathematical insights he had long kept private. Explaining advanced concepts to her attentive mind revived dormant passions. He began delving into esoteric theorems with renewed zeal, gathering reference texts to enrich their discussions.

Rajesh found solace in mentoring this gifted student, seeing the gleam of comprehension in her eyes. It awakened dormant purpose, reminding him that though one light had faded, his role as teacher remained. He still had knowledge and wisdom to impart, kindled by experiences that shaped him.

Aditi absorbed all eagerly, countering with deep questions that pushed Rajesh to illuminate opaque ideas in new ways. Her gratitude and enthusiasm for learning kindled pride in his mentorship. On walks home after tutoring, Rajesh felt fulfilled, reviving seeds planted long ago.

"You remind me why I do this," he told Aditi softly one evening. "To see bright minds blossom and carry knowledge forward gives meaning to it all." She replied with a smile, "Then let our talks continue as long as you are willing, sir. You have so much left to teach." Her faith reawakened Rajesh's sense of purpose anew each day.

# CHAPTER FIFTEEN

# Light Ahead

Rajesh walked to the university, breathing in the warm morning air. The sunlight enveloped the landscape in a gentle glow as his students' laughter echoed in the distance. He reflected on how far he had come.

Through conversation with Aditi, he had found solace in remembering Leah with joy rather than pain. Her memory was no longer a burden, but rather a blessing - a reminder of love's power to uplift even in life's darkest hours.

Stepping into the lecture hall, Rajesh saw Aditi deep in discussion with classmates. Her inquisitive nature and passion for scholarship shone through. Smiling to himself, he began the day's lesson, sharing knowledge with the calm assurance of one at peace.

No longer was he the man haunted by shadows of his past. Rajesh had made amends with memory and found purpose anew: to nurture young minds as Aditi had nurtured his spirit back to health. Her empathy taught him that even broken hearts may mend, learning compassion's lessons in the tender hands of a friend.

Rajesh paused beside Aditi as the others filed out of class. "Your insight never ceases to surprise me," he smiled.

"Learning from you has been the true gift," she replied shyly. An unfamiliar flutter rose in Rajesh's chest at her words.

That evening, Aditi brought freshly baked bread to share. They walked the riverbank together, lost in lively scholarship. But beneathdiscussion of theorem and text lay an blossoming intimacy - a delicate bond that eased loneliness and filled emptiness where shadows had dwelled too long.

Was it fate they had found one another? Or chance alone? Looking into Aditi's eyes, Rajesh sensed a solace deeper than friendship. Her patience and care had guided him from grief's shadows into light's gentle embrace.

Now, as dusk's colors melted into star-speckled night, he sensed dormant parts of himself reawaken in Aditi's quiet company. Did she feel it too - this kinship of soul that defied simple reason? For now, it was enough that she stood beside him, helping write hope upon affliction's page.

As mornings turned crisp with approaching winter, Rajesh and Aditi took to walking together by the river. One afternoon, she paused to watch leaves dance upon the current.

"All things must change," Aditi said softly. "Even sorrows, in time, lose hold on the heart they once burdened."

Rajesh looked at her thoughtful face, finding solace in every word. "You give me courage to face what comes - and to let go what clings too tightly still," he said.

She met his gaze, and for a moment unspoken understanding flowed between them - that the present held promise unknown. Might comfort blossom from companionship in a way he'd not thought to feel again?

As darkness fell, Rajesh walked Aditi home under faint stars. At her door, shy pulses of feeling stirred strangely within - Hope, once distant, now growing nearer if he dared reach for what lay beyond grief's heavy shroud. Aditi smiled gently, words unneeded between them, and clasped his hand in silent care and guidance into a future waiting to unfold.

At dawn one morning, Rajesh stood quietly before Leah's memorial - a young tree tended with care. He breathed deep, letting silence speak.

Your light showed me beauty's life-changing power, Leah. Through you, I found strength beyond myself. Our love was singular - a gift I'll always treasure. Now, others need the care you gave so selflessly.

Leah's memory stirred no pain, only gratitude. With Aditi's guidance, he'd made peace with dark days past. Now, looking to a future still unwritten, he sensed her blessing on whatever lay ahead.

Dearest heart, though you walk other shores, your spirit lives within all who strive as we did, side by side, for wisdom's beckoning call. I'll carry you in my soul's silent moments as a reminder of life's meaning. Farewell, my friend - till memory's sweet leaves we meet again.

Rajesh smiled quietly, turning to greet the dawn. In its glow, the past's shadows lifted to reveal hope - and a journey whose secrets lay in love's gentle hands.,

Each morning, Rajesh walked to campus smiling to himself. Within lecture halls' walls lay purpose rediscovered - to see sparks of curiosity catch light in young minds.

Here, among scholars seeking knowledge as he once did, shadows from sorrow's chapter fell away. For his students, he felt a protectiveness akin to family; in their eagerness to learn, he found reflection of the drive that brought him here from village roots.

None brought him joy more than Aditi, whose probing questions cut to insight's heart. Together they wandered theorems' uncharted corners, forging new paths guided by passion, not prestige. Her friendship's steady light pointed hopeward when darkness crept near.

More than mentor, she had become solace and strength - reminding him that in life's most difficult terrain, two sets of footprints need not travel alone. As seasons turned, their bond grew roots of care, trust and compassion deep enough to nurture whatever blossoms fate held in store.

Now, looking to a future guided by friendship, faith and forgiveness, Rajesh walked in peace, grateful life had brought him from shadows to this place of purpose under promise of a new dawn., As dawn light spilled over fields, Rajesh and Aditi walked the winding path home. Much had changed since hardship's heavy curtain fell, he reflected - and more transformation lay ahead, unknown.

Yet facing each new day, he felt steady; anchored by friendships seeded in life's hardest soil. Now, having glimpsed darkness' harsh lessons, Rajesh held fast to hope that even bitter waters lead to wisdoms alleviating sorrow.

Though clouds still gathered at horizon's edge promising storms, in Aditi's smile he sensed sunlight's promise to broke through in time. Each dawn was a blessing - to see familiar landscapes made new through companionship, teaching joys rediscovered and service of a greater good.

Now grounded in forgiveness and with scars healed by kindness, Rajesh walked assured, believing light may emerge when least expected after darkest nights. And holding fast to friendship, faith and future's mysteries, he met each sunrise with quiet optimism that whatever lay ahead would hold rewards for having weathered hardship's refining fire.

Their footprints in damp earth faded, but memories lingered of a journey showing that even broken hearts may rise and, in caring hands, bloom anew. Hope was rekindled, and with it, belief that life holds beauty enough for all if lived embracing life's simple lessons of love, compassion - and gratitude for each dawn lighting a way forward. As evening fell, Rajesh looked out at fields fading to shadows. He turned to Aditi beside him.

"The new term begins soon. I've decided to accept that invitation - to teach for a season in America." Life was blessedly long, but each moment fleeting. No longer would he take days for granted or push aside dreams whose times had come.

Aditi smiled warmly. "Your students there will be very lucky indeed. And I look forward to reading the letters and papers you'll send." She knew his restless mind and scholar's soul craved new frontiers of thought.

Rajesh nodded. "And once I've stretched my wings abroad awhile, there are so many places I've yet to see through these weary eyes - journeys to take, thoughts to set to page. No more hidden from life's beauty."

Days, months and years stretched ahead, rich with promise. Rajesh felt renewed purpose to embrace each dawn, learn from dark and light, seek wisdom - and, in love and laughter shared with kindred souls, live fully in time freely given. His was a bounty of thanksgivings, and for them he sent up prayers of praise into deepening night. As morning's light spilled warmth upon the lands, Rajesh stood watching day break through misty fields. Much had changed since sorrow held him in its grasping thrall.

Now within his breast, shadows' tight grip had loosened, leaving space for hopes nurtured through struggle into fragile shoots of beauty. Each dawn was a blessing, like pages of a life lived fully. And in this new soft light he sensed the promise of mysteries awaiting.

What adventures lay beyond today's gentle hours? What

insights would compassion's lessons unveil through seasons yet to be lived? Smiling softly, Rajesh sent up a prayer of thanks for life's turnings - both bitter and sweet.

With heart now open to each gift, he went gladly to greet students gathering in dawn's glow, ready to walk with them on scholarship's unfurling path. For having weathered darkness, Rajesh knew life held reward enough if lived embracing love, service, forgiveness...and gratitude for a sun every morn that illuminated each step of a journey whose end remained unseen, unfolding still in hope's quiet grace.

# Author's Note

As we come to the end of this journey, I want to express my deepest gratitude to each reader who has embarked on this adventure with Rajesh. Your presence on this literary odyssey means more to me than words can convey.

This book is not just a tale; it is a shared experience. I hope you found resonance in Rajesh's journey, the trials he faced, the love that guided him, and the dreams that fueled his spirit. In telling this story, I aimed to celebrate the enduring human spirit, the power of connections, and the transformative nature of dreams.

Let's stay in touch! email me for updates on upcoming projects, events, and more.
Email: pspnandi@gmail.com